JESUS & MARY

Jon Ferguson

Huge Jam Publishing, 2022
www.hugejam.com

DEDICATION

To my mother Ester Golda Israelsen Ferguson
who showered me with love

If a tiny omniscient insect crawled into your ear one cozy star-filled night and whispered, "Friend of this world, I must tell you that there are no historical facts," would this change anything about your life? If the insect then decided to stay a while and explain what it meant, would you listen? Would you care to hear what it meant? Would you let the insect metamorphose your whole view of the very idea of "history"? Would you let the insect scratch your eardrum with its tiny hands and feet until you understood what it meant? Most people would never understand, but for those who would, here is a story of Jesus and Mary Magdalene.

PREFACE

Everything ever written about Mary Magdalene is false. Everything ever written about Jesus is false. Everything ever written about history is false for history is not a ball of string that unwinds in a straight line for people to touch, see, and understand. Every moment is infinitely complex. Everything is attached to everything else. How many moments has history had? How much Being is in every moment? There is not enough time and not enough words to describe any single moment of history. When anybody tries to explain anything they are trying to squeeze the universe into their own glass jar. Anyone who claims he can do this is a charlatan, gentle or otherwise.

The life of the man they call Jesus is a very good example. What does anyone really know about Jesus? He was said to be the son of God. What does anyone know about God? He was said to be born of a virgin mother. No one knows if this is true. No one knows anything about his mother's sex life. Anyone could say his mother was a virgin. I had a cousin who got pregnant and her devout Christian parents said she never had sex, but that an errant sperm had crept inside her vagina. Was this "true"?

You and I are alive today. Does anybody really know anything about us? Does anyone understand the inter-workings of the millions of atoms and cells that we are "made of"? Of course not. And our hearts and minds? Even people who live with us don't have a clue as to what transpires in the depths of our souls. The world is a gargantuan secret. Jesus lived two thousand years ago. Think of how his life has been warped by millions of interpretations that have nothing to do with the truth. Nobody will ever know the truth. People just use other people to fit their version of the truth. People use "history" to fit their version of what life is all about. But there is no knowable history, and life can never fit into that glass jar.

My story of the love affair between Mary Magdalene and Jesus is what I imagine happened. Nobody has to agree with me. I don't want any followers. I don't want to start a new religion or destroy an old one. More lies have probably been told about Jesus than any other person who has ever walked the earth. There are hundreds of versions of his life. Most people will buy into the version that confirms what they happen to believe about life and truth. I don't believe in Christianity, but sometimes I like to believe in Jesus. Like Nietzsche said, "There was only one Christian and he died on the cross."

Le voici…

ONE

There are no books except a few copies of the Old Testament written on parchment. There are no newspapers, televisions, radios, magazines, iPads, or phones. Computers, cameras, cars, trains, airplanes, bicycles, and electric light bulbs will be invented a couple of thousand years later. There are no vaccinations against diseases and medicine men have absolutely no idea about what goes on under the skin. No one has ever heard of a gun or a bomb. All wars are fought face to face. People don't know that a baby is made when a sperm penetrates an egg. Most men die before the age of forty, women before thirty. The world is flat and not much bigger than Liechtenstein. Few people have been more than a few miles from where they were born. Nobody has heard of an atom or a cell. Leibnitz won't be born for seventeen centuries. The word gravity means nothing. There are no sharp needles with which to sew clothes. One pair of shoes is a lot. You bathe in a river or a lake or the sea. Only the sun heats the water. There is no toilet paper. For that matter, there are no toilets. No one has ever heard of a Pope, a Catholic, a Crusade, a Muslim, a Mormon, a Christian, an Evolution or a Big Bang. Olives are a food staple. People get born in mangers. No one calls the area around Jerusalem "holy".

There is a lot going on elsewhere on the planet earth, but the people in and around Jerusalem don't know about it. The people in the other parts of the earth don't know about Jerusalem.

TWO

That's just the way it was back then. A few thousand years down the road, today will look the same.

THREE

Isn't it interesting how the farther away myths and traditions get, the more people believe them. Shortly after Jesus died, nobody believed he was God's son or a miracle worker. Nobody believed he died to save the world from sin. Most people didn't have a clue about what sin was. They were just trying to survive. Sure there was the Jewish tradition and the Old Testament. But the Romans had most of the power. They wielded the big sticks. As they slowly self-destructed and whittled themselves away, the whole Christian thing started to take root. But it had no roots when Jesus died.

FOUR

Forget the wise men and the virgin. Jesus was born like every other kid, on a straw bed. His mother was nervous but loving. His father had a pleasant disposition, a bad leg, and tendency toward laziness. Jesus's childhood was normal: no broken arms or legs, lots of bread and olives, stories about Adam and Eve and the Ten Commandments. He was special because he had an inquisitive mind. He tended to doubt much of what he heard. He asked lots of questions. When they said Moses made the Red Sea open up, he thought it probably never happened. When they said God made the world in six days, then rested, he thought they had no proof. If God were Almighty why would He even need to rest? Why six days? Why didn't He have slaves do the work like the Romans did? And he knew the Romans had other stories and other gods to explain where everybody came from. When he reached age sixteen, he had no idea about what was true and false. He just looked at the world and observed the life that was in front of him: blue sky, sun, hills, paths, people, moon, goats, cats, dogs, stars, insects, trees, flowers, grass, rain, clouds, suffering, pain, laughter, birth, death, happiness, sadness. When he saw a creature die, it didn't look like it was going anywhere.

What was the sky? What was that vast sheet of blue, grey, and black above him? What was in it? At night, what glittered? He took walks. He wondered why, and how, and what. He had no answers. Sometimes the moon was bigger than other times. Were there two moons? Three? Four? Sometimes it was a half-circle. Sometimes just a slice. He got dizzy. People told him it wasn't worth getting dizzy about. God created it. But Jesus doubted God, any and all gods. The Romans had lots of them. How big was it all? Did it end?

When he was seventeen he started watching himself think. Did thinking happen in the eye, the head, the ears, the heart, the groin? Maybe it came from every part of the body. Maybe God put thoughts in people's heads. Maybe the thinking invented God. Did animals think? In any case a lot of thoughts came out of people's mouths. He listened to what people said. Most of what they said had to do with themselves. That made some kind of sense.

Jesus was friends with everybody — Pharisees,

Romans, slaves, old, young, men, women, children, animals. He wandered a lot and watched the world. Everybody had his or her story to tell. He was a good listener. His world was small. Stories overlapped and intertwined. The same words and people came up over and over again.

Jesus's mother and father were both dead before he was eleven. His mother died first, at the age of twenty-nine, after giving birth to a girl, a half-sister. His father was much older than his mother. He had had two other children with another woman before fathering Jesus. He died an old man at age fifty-seven.

Back then kids weren't babied like they are today. You had to fend for yourself early. Which reminds me of something I read in a history book the other day. Did you know that in the twelfth century there was something called "The Children's Crusade"? 30,000 children between the ages of six and twelve were walking together across what is now France to get to Jerusalem. When they arrived in Marseille they were put in boats. Two of the boats sank and everyone on them died. The other boats went to Northern Africa where the children were all sold off as slaves.

FIVE

Mary is seventeen, twelve years younger than Jesus. Her eyes are small turquoise oceans that see much of the same world Jesus sees. (Jesus didn't see the uncle or the Roman soldier who came to rape her.) Males are moved when she walks by. Her clothes are like sacks; men try to see through them. She has been on her own since she was seven, sleeping and eating wherever she can. At first she was like a wild animal, only seeing out and seeking to survive. Now she has started to reflect and she loves Jesus. She wonders what moves heads and hearts, particularly her own. She eventually wonders what moves everything — moon, sun, fish, snake, bird, finger, foot, cloud, Roman, uncle, donkey, tree…

Over the years they have crossed paths many times, but neither she nor Jesus has ever dared or wanted to stop. But on this day when they see each other their eyes stick. Does it matter why? He knows her name is Mary like his mother's. His head is slightly tilted as he walks toward her to speak. "Mary, I have finished my work for the day. Would you like to walk with me?"

They leave the village and climb a hill to a place where they can look out over the land. It is early evening and the sun is behind them. When she speaks, he is reminded of trees in the wind…

I know a little about you. Your father was Joseph.

Yes. He is dead.

You seem to have lots of friends. Every time I see you, you have people around you.

I am nice to people. I see no reason to treat people badly.

Even the Romans?

The Romans didn't ask to be Romans. They're only doing their job.

I wish they would do it elsewhere.

Someone will always have power. What's more important is the power you have over yourself.

When they rape you your power gets lost.

They shouldn't rape you, but "shouldn't" is a word that doesn't have much meaning.

They are pigs.

Men are animals.

Worse.

Not always.

Of course.

Have they raped you?

Once. A soldier followed me to where I was sleeping. I woke up in the middle of the night and he was lying next to me. I smelled him before I saw him. He told me not to make noise and everything would be all right. I hate the Romans. I'm lucky it's only happened once with them.

Has it happened with anyone else?

My uncle. He isn't really my uncle. He is my half-brother. I call him my uncle because he's fifteen years older than me. He's also your brother.

What do you mean?

Your half-brother. He's your father's son.

How do you know?

My mother told me that Joseph fathered David then left her. She was young. Younger than I am now.

How old are you?

Seventeen.

I know this David. My father never told me he was my brother.

In the end we're all brothers and sisters.

And David, did he rape you?

He forced himself on me. I was fifteen, the same age as my mother was when she had Joseph's baby.

But there was no baby?

No.

And the Roman soldier? There was no baby?

No.

So, you are not a prostitute? I'd been told that

sometimes you sell your body.

All women are prostitutes. That is, all women who make love when they don't want to are prostitutes. If they don't do it for money they do it for a home, security, family, food…It's the same thing.

And you?

I've given my body for coins when I was hungry.

I can't imagine making love to a woman who didn't want to make love with me.

You must be lucky then and have women who want you. She looked away from him when she said this and stared out into the desert.

Not recently…he mused. And I really don't understand people who do things against other people's wills.

Wills often collide. Most men don't think before they act.

Fools know not what they do.

Why do you think God lets bad things happen?

What is bad for one is good for another.

Why would God let men kill each other?

If He existed, I don't think He would.

You don't think He exists?

I have no idea. But if He does exist and He lets people rape you, He is a strange God.

The Jewish God is very strange, destroying lots of things, getting mad and throwing His thunderbolts.

That's why I only pretend I'm a Jew. I really don't believe in any of it.

You don't believe in heaven and hell?

I can't believe God would punish people. The idea of hell is barbaric. The Jews try to frighten people to get them to follow their rules. Why would God want to frighten people? I can only imagine a god trying to help people. Like a mother or a good father.

Maybe God isn't nice. The Romans have many gods and some of them are cruel.

Yes, I know.

Jesus, do you think there's the one single god…or many gods?

How could anyone know?

But people pretend to know. Why?

Because they can't help themselves. Their minds are small. Are you thirsty? There's a stream not far from here.

Yes, actually I am.

Let's go then.

As they rose he took her hand.

SIX

Mary and Jesus saw each other the next day. It was the Sabbath. Friday? Saturday? Sunday? What difference does it make? The universe has no idea what day it is. Nobody knows when the earth's spinning started. But we sure like to think we do.

SEVEN

If you wish to have any chance of understanding what this book is trying to say, you must remove all preconceived ideas about Jesus based on your own twentieth or twenty-first century life. Most people in the Occident concoct their idea of Jesus from what goes on (or went on) in their church and on two major holidays, Christmas and Easter. Let's forget Easter for now and think about the way we imagine Jesus based on our celebration of his birth every year on the twenty-fifth of December:

First we see the Virgin Mary, her nice quiet husband Joseph, and the little baby Jesus in Mary's arms all warm and cozy in an open barn, with a hay-filled manger. Everybody is happy and healthy. Jesus never cries and Mary looks like she just dressed after a warm bath. There is no doctor in sight, but there are three wise men (why are they wise? – what wise things have they ever said? – of course we have no idea about any of that) who have brought wonderful gifts. Then we see the heavenly star above the blessed stable shining divine light on the whole scene. This is how we perceive the birth of Jesus. Then we add the Christmas tree in the living room with all the lights, candles, glittering balls and tinsel. Now throw in the presents under the tree, many bought and wrapped with much thought and love. On top of that add the best meal of the year that mother has spent all day preparing. And finally turn on the stereo and hear some of the most beautiful peaceful songs ever written sung by the amazing voices of Bing Crosby, Mahalia Jackson, Johnny Mathis, Barbara Hendricks, Placido Domingo, or the Mormon Tabernacle Choir…This is CHRISTmas — the glorious concept shines in your head for the rest of your life!

You will never be able to dissociate the Christmas holiday from your idea of Jesus. But this idea has absolutely nothing to do with the birth and life of Jesus. It is total myth. Nobody is suggesting that myths are bad. They might be the most necessary things in human society. But they have nothing to do with truth and what actually happened in the world.

Jesus was probably born with great pain to the mother. There was no special star above the barn. There were no wise men coming on camels in the moonlight. (Maybe Jesus was born at ten o'clock in the morning.) Joseph might have been nowhere in sight.

No one will ever know the circumstances of Jesus's birth. But it most surely has nothing to do with the atmosphere of Christmas as we celebrate it today.

Now think of the Jesus that we hear about in our Christian churches. Think of the painted pictures on the walls. Jesus always has that nice beard and flowing clean long hair. Probably every man in Jesus's time had a beard and nobody had clean hair. Then the stories of Jesus, the miracles, the walking on water, feeding five thousand people with a few loaves of bread, healing lepers and other people stuck with pathetic lives. None of this is likely any truer than the myths about Jesus's birth. We must wipe all this from our heads and try to clean the slate.

Who was Jesus? What was the world like two thousand years ago? We'll never know, but we're trying to imagine as best we can. Remember, Jesus's world was small, like Rhode Island, and flat. No one had a clue what was going on over the rest of the planet. Just like us today…we have no idea what is going on in the rest of the universe. Jesus's universe was Nazareth, Jerusalem, Galilee, Bethlehem, the sky directly overhead, and nothing else. Nobody had a clue where any of it came from. Nobody in Jesus's world had been to Africa, America, China, even Turkey, Greece, or Europe. They hadn't even been to Syria, Egypt, or Iraq. Our universe is Earth, Mars, Jupiter, the Milky Way, 13,000,000,000 years of evolution, black holes, and a few more galaxies. Nobody knows what's really out there – way out there! Or how long it's been there. 2,000 years from now – the same amount of calendar time we are from Jesus – people will have a totally different view of life and the universe.

It's all about perspective. We have ours. Jesus had his. Back to his…

EIGHT

Jesus and Mary met again in the olive grove on the hill overlooking Nazareth. Though it was the Sabbath neither went into the synagogue before or after their rendezvous. Jesus didn't believe he needed a rabbi to tell him what was good or bad, right or wrong, true or false. As far as he was concerned the rabbis didn't know any more than he did about anything. They thought their thoughts, he thought his. Also, he didn't like crowds of people. He never wanted others to speak or act for him, especially not a mob. He had seen many times how mobs became violent and thoughtless. Remember, Jesus was a doubter and a thinker. He was also twenty-nine years old. He'd had time to wonder, wander, marvel, and think about his world.

As they sat in the sunburnt grass under the olive

tree, Jesus noticed how beautiful Mary Magdalene was. She was seventeen. Though she had been raped twice (actually many more times if you consider all the times she let men have her in order to get something to eat), her face showed no signs or scars of misery or suffering. Only every now and then Jesus would notice a vertical crease appear above her nose which might reveal some small hint of worry or dismay. Her skin was like the petal of a flower, he thought. When she talked, she would often wet her lips between sentences. All he wanted to do was kiss her, but he didn't because he didn't want to be like other men who had precipitously thrown themselves on her because of her beauty. He could wait forever because he loved her.

Where's your mother?

I don't know. She went away with a man when I was too young to remember. I don't know if the man forced her to go or not. She left me with her sister, who died when I was nine or ten. I'm not sure exactly. I was left to fend for myself. For years I was like a stray dog just trying to find food and a place to sleep. I often slept next to that rock over there (she points with a long, lovely finger on her left hand).

Jesus rejoined. *I was fortunate. When my mother died, I still had my father and eventually he gave me work. He was rather lazy, so he was happy when I was old enough to do things for him.*

What was his work?

He made tables and chairs and cupboards. I must have started working when I was eleven. I still work sometimes as I need money to eat. I sleep in the same house I've always slept in. It's one room, but the roof over it is strong and rain never gets in. You must see it one day.

I would like to. Do you have children? Do you live alone?

I have no children that I know of. There are travelers who sometimes stay with me, but not for long. And you, Mary…Do you have children?

I was with child once, I think. I was sick in the morning for a few weeks. Then something happened. I bled a lot and whatever was inside me was gone.

You said you were "like a stray dog."

Yes, I was.

One thing that fascinates me is the differences – or lack of differences – between men and animals. What qualities do men have that animals don't have? And what qualities do animals have that men don't have? How are we alike? How are we different?

It depends on which man and which animal. I have known men who act like animals and I've seen animals that appear to act like men. Both men and animals can be gentle. Both men and animals can be cruel and violent.

I am fascinated by birds. No man can fly. No man can pass from tree to tree without putting his feet back on the ground.

Do you think God created animals for man?

Who's even to say God created animals? Maybe animals created God. Maybe neither was created? I have no idea.

All the rabbis say God created man, then animals, then plants and trees.

What do the rabbis know?

I don't know.

And what might this god they talk about be? They talk about God as if he were their best friend. As if they know what He is like and how He acts. Maybe God is nothing like they describe. Maybe there is no God. They have never seen this God. Maybe their God has a god over Him. Maybe birds are the real gods. Mary, for me it is all a big mystery, bigger than any mind can imagine. Mary takes Jesus's hand and holds it to her breast.

I've never heard anyone talk that way before, Jesus.

And I have never had anyone listen the way you listen, Mary. Few people want to hear me.

I will hear you.

And I will hear you, Jesus said.

NINE

Both Mary and Jesus took the long way home after they separated. Jesus had brought a loaf of bread and some olives and they had drunk wine. Both had finished eating for the day. There was about an hour of sunlight left. Before going to sleep each wanted to be alone with the thought of the other. When a body fills with love the rest of the human world can be a great cacophony.

Mary lived with a woman who had four children – all girls between the ages of six and twelve – and a dying old man. The woman said the man was her father. She said that years ago her husband had been beaten by the Romans for refusing to give them the family donkey. The soldiers took the husband away, but "miraculously" left the donkey. For the past six months Mary had been sleeping in the departed husband's bed. Every morning, except the Sabbath, she would feed and wash the old man while the woman and her daughters went to the market to sell the vegetables that grow behind the house. The donkey transported the goods.

As she walked on the path on the edge of the town, Mary was so engrossed in her thoughts about the man she had spent the afternoon with that she didn't look behind her to see if she was being followed. She had three thoughts spinning through her mind. Firstly, "Is it possible that there is no god who created and rules over the earth?" Secondly, "If there is no god in heaven, must I find a god on earth?" Thirdly, "Jesus is not like other men. He could be my god on earth and I could be his goddess...for as long as we live."

Fortunately, no one was following her. She got home just as darkness enveloped Nazareth. The woman was concerned about her. The girls were already asleep in their corner of the hut.

Mary, I was worried about you.

I'm completely fine. In fact, I had a wonderful afternoon.

Have you eaten enough?

Yes, thank you. But I'd like some water. I have walked a long way.

Of course. There is enough for tonight and the morning.

I was with the man named Jesus. Do you know him?

Yes, I do know who he is. I have seen him in the market. He is kind, but very strange. Sometimes he buys vegetables and then immediately gives them away to the poor.

We spent the afternoon talking. He says things I've never heard another man say. He doesn't believe in the Jewish God. He doesn't believe there is a heaven or a hell. He thinks that when you die that is the end. He says life is a mystery, but it is very possible that this life is all we have.

How can a man not believe in God or heaven or hell? He is a Jew, isn't he?

He says there is no reason to believe the rabbis.

Then who should we believe? The Romans…?

No, not the Romans. But he doesn't hate them. He says they're only doing their job and that they did not ask to be born Roman. What they do is not their fault. He says if Jews had been born Romans, they'd be doing the same things.

The Romans are stupid.

Jesus thinks everybody is stupid. Not stupid in a bad way. But stupid like animals.

Did he try to take advantage of your body?

No, not for a second. It was I who pulled his hand to my breast. I was the first to touch his flesh.

I don't believe you Mary.

It's true. We were alone in the olive orchard. We talked. We listened to each other. I've never had such a conversation. I've never felt such things in the presence of a man.

He cannot be a good man if he doesn't believe in God.

But so many bad men believe in God. The Romans believe in God.

They believe in gods…the wrong gods. They don't believe in Jehovah.

Why are the Roman gods wrong and the Jewish god right? That's the kind of question Jesus would ask…

The Romans are bad and the Jews are good.

Jesus would say that "good" and "bad" mean very different things in different mouths. He doesn't judge people. He says no one asked to be who they are… nothing…no man, no animal, no tree, no flower.

Mary, I think he is dangerous. You must be careful. Men who are different are dangerous.

Not this man.

Are you sure?

Is one ever sure? But Jesus is like no man I have ever met. I think I love him.

The old man was listening in his corner of the room. The two women had thought he was asleep. It was now totally dark outside. A small candle was burning on the table. The old man spoke: *I have been listening to you. How can a man who is gentle with a beautiful young woman like Mary be dangerous? As I lay dying, I too often wonder if there is a god. How could there be so much suffering if there was an almighty god? Why would God let people be killed by diseases and wars and be left to suffer in their death beds?*

The woman replied: *God punishes those who are evil.*

Have I been evil? I have never tried to harm anyone in my life. Yet I am suffering every minute of every day. Why doesn't God punish the Romans who steal our money and conquer our land?

God's ways are not man's ways.

How do you know?

The rabbis teach it.

Why do the rabbis know? People follow the rabbis because they have to follow somebody. The rabbis follow other rabbis. Nobody knows if what the rabbis say is true. But nobody dares say what they teach is false. Mary's friend Jesus sounds as though he is not a follower. He is not somebody's sheep.

Mary spoke softly: *No, he isn't.*

I would like to meet him and talk to him. Could you bring him here one day before I die?

Surely. I will ask him tomorrow. We are meeting again in the olive orchard.

Be careful Mary, the woman said. *He could be dangerous.*

TEN

Just imagine, no one really knows what language Jesus spoke. If you comb through history books, there is no consensus as to whether Jesus spoke Aramaic, Latin, Hebrew, or even a little Greek. In any case, languages come and go and get transformed. In the end, they are only sounds humans make. We have a tendency to think they reveal truth or falsehood. But do they? Jesus thought languages simplify everything. They take the great mystery of life and try to give it sense, meaning, and make it understandable. Jesus knew man would never understand. He used language like he walked: delicately, trying not to kill or damage things underfoot.

For our purposes, it doesn't matter what language Jesus and Mary spoke together. In the end, what they really created was their own language, a language of a love, the kind that has rarely existed on the face of the earth.

ELEVEN

Good morning Jesus.

How are you Mary?

Seeing you in the cool of the Sabbath morning is beautiful. I love the morning when the sun appears again. In the middle of the night, I often fear the sun will take a different path…run away and never come back and we will live in eternal darkness. I've had many dreams about this.

The sun is the earth's dearest friend. Neither will abandon the other.

You know Sabbath is the only morning I can see you because all the other mornings have me tending to the old man. Today his daughter's taking care of him as there's no market for her to go to.

Yes, I know. You've told me. It's why I'll start loving the Sabbath again.

You don't like the Sabbath, Jesus?

My dear Mary, why should the Sabbath be any different from any other day? If there is a god that deserves our worship, we should be thankful to Him every minute of every day. Why do the priests choose just one day a week where everyone pretends they are righteous? And I hate all this talk about heaven and hell and the hereafter. The kingdom of God should be here and now…on this earth…every moment we are alive.

Yes.

And I have come to dislike all the priests and rabbis that talk about good and evil and sin and salvation. No man has the right to judge another man. Only an all-knowing god could be in a position to judge.

I think the priests judge others so that they can feel good about themselves. They must call others sinners so they can call themselves righteous.

I love your voice, Mary, and what you say. I stopped going to the synagogue years ago. I would ask questions like "How do you know this or that is true?" and they would tell me to fast and pray and I would know. Well, I fasted and I prayed and nothing happened. They would say I hadn't fasted and prayed enough.

What precisely did you ask Jesus? I have had many questions, but I never dared ask them.

Many people have questions that they don't dare ask. They are afraid of the priests. I am afraid of no priest.

So tell me about your questions…before I kiss you.

Jesus and Mary both laughed. For many days now, Jesus had wanted to kiss Mary, but had not dared to be the one to instigate their first embrace. He knew that many men had thrown themselves upon Mary. He didn't want to be another such man. He wanted their first kiss to come from her.

And it would come in a few minutes. Mary would take Jesus's hand and then their four lips would become one. But first Jesus would talk about his questions.

I had dozens and dozens of questions, Mary. They started filling my head when I was twelve or thirteen years old. Questions like: If God created the earth, who created God? Why do the Romans and Greeks have many gods and the Jews only one? When we pray, how do we know God is listening? Why would God allow so much suffering? How do we know that the thoughts that fill our heads correspond to the truth of the world…? And then I would look at the sky and wonder: Is our world really the center of the universe like the rabbis say? What…what is out there in that deep blue sky? Nothing? Other worlds? Different worlds? Different creatures and different gods? And those stars that fill the sky when the sun disappears… Where do they come from? How far away are they? Do they have wings? Do they fly? Are we flying? If there is a god, what would he or she or it be like? Maybe God is very different from man…maybe God has no interest in man at all...or maybe God created nothing...a shepherd didn't create his sheep...perhaps God is a Shepherd who found men and decided to take care of them...maybe there is no God...maybe man is God but just doesn't know it...maybe man must become God...Oh Mary, I had so many questions passing through my head. The teachers all thought I was crazy.

Jesus had been sitting on the grass. He slowly extended his body and lay flat on his back. He stared at the sky, then closed his eyes. That is when Mary kissed him, at first very gently. But soon they would be rolling in the grass, their lips and bodies powerful magnets.

Minutes went by. When their bodies finally separated, there was a moment of silence until Jesus spoke again.

Mary, what if everything the Jews say is untrue? What if everything the Romans say is untrue? What if no one knows what the truth of the world is? I have tried to pray hundreds of times. I prayed to the Jewish god. I prayed to the Roman gods. I got no answers that I could say were answers. I think any answers I got just came from my own head.

You're an honest man Jesus.

I try to be, but one never knows if one is being honest with oneself or not.

At least you try to be honest.

Maybe honesty isn't even a virtue. Maybe power is

the only thing that counts.

But power is certainly not a virtue. The Roman soldiers, the ones who have overpowered me and used my body are not virtuous. They are wild animals.

Maybe all men are wild animals. Maybe women are too…just a different kind of animal. The rabbis all say that God created man in His own image. If they're lying, then in whose image was he created?

Maybe he was not created.

I have thought that so many times. At first the thought was a frightening one. It's hard to imagine mankind with no link to a god. But it is possible, Mary. As I look at all the suffering and stupidity in the world, I begin to believe that it is truly possible. Sometimes everything looks so strange and barbaric.

But there are beautiful things too.

Like you.

Like flowers and butterflies and some of the fish in the sea.

Mary and Jesus lay silent again. They touched and kissed again. Both felt like they had never felt before. Jesus had lain with other women many times, but none had ever felt like Mary and he had never felt as he now did in Mary's arms. Mary felt her body tingle and parts of her seemed like they were melting, stone to liquid.

But they did not make love on this day. They would talk some more and make love for the first time another day.

I have often asked the gods what the purpose of life

is. How should a man spend his time on earth? But most people are slaves. These questions mean nothing to them, just like they mean nothing to animals. The donkey that carries goods to the market doesn't think about what the purpose of his life should be. That purpose is imposed by his master. It is the same for most people. They do what the rich and the Romans say. They have no time to think about anything except working, eating, drinking, and sleeping. It's not their fault that they haven't time to think. I have been lucky. I've had time to think. But is thinking necessarily good? Maybe thinking makes a person crazy.

You're not crazy Jesus. You're not like the man who cries and rolls in the street.

Maybe every head is different. But most heads don't ask a lot of questions. Most heads are satisfied with very simple answers. They accept what they are told by whoever is in power. They accept what the rabbis and the Romans say. They accept the traditions they are born into. They follow the herd like sheep. But I could never do that. Even as a boy.

Mary rubbed Jesus's chest with her hand. He stared at the sky with brown wide-open eyes. She kissed his neck, then spoke.

Jesus, how much have you thought about the word "love"?

Enough to know what it isn't.

Enough to define it?

I imagine everyone's definition would be a little

different.

How does one know if one loves another person?
One doesn't know. One feels it.
Can we trust what we feel?
What else is there to trust?
Do you think animals love each other?
I don't know, but I love animals.
Most animals die too quickly.
Who is to say what is long and what is short?
A minute can be long and a year can be short.
That is one of the mysteries.

They both looked at the sky while the sky looked at them.

Do you think there are any answers, Jesus?

There are more answers than there are questions. But most questions are badly phrased and most answers are empty and learned by rote. The world is such a mysterious place.

Not when we're in each other's arms.

Maybe that is when it is most mysterious, Mary. They both laughed and rolled in the grass. This time Mary had brought some olives and bread and a few pieces of fruit. Jesus had the jug of wine.

Before going home Mary asked Jesus when he might be able to come and see the old man. He said he would come the next morning when she was caring for him.

TWELVE

The old man's eyes opened when he heard Jesus walk into the room. He tried to sit up in his bed of straw. Jesus motioned for him to stay calm, pushed a stool to the side of the bed and sat down. Mary went outside.

Mary has spoken about you often, Jesus. Thank you for coming.

And she has told me about you. I wanted to meet you.

I am a dying man, Jesus. I will soon be gone. What do you think happens when a person dies?

I'll be honest. I have no idea. Life and death are both mysteries. I'm not even convinced that life and death are opposites.

What do you mean?

I'm not sure if life is one thing and death is another. Maybe all things are tied together.

The rabbis speak of heaven and hell. Do you think there is a heaven...and a hell filled with fire and damnation?

The rabbis have no idea. No one has any idea. No dead man has ever returned to the land of the living.

But the rabbis have their sacred books...

How do we know they are sacred? The Romans have their sacred books too. But are they sacred? If one is sacred, the other is not.

Yes... (The old man hesitated. It was difficult for him to speak.) *Jesus, I want to ask you about a dream I once had. I want to tell you about it and then have you tell me what you think.*

Let me hear your dream.

I will try to describe it as clearly as possible...I was in my mother's womb with my twin brother.

Did you have a twin brother?

Yes, but he died shortly after we were born...We were together in the womb. Our world was dark and liquid like that of fish in the bottom of the sea. I said to my brother, "Do you think there is life after we leave this womb?" "No," he said. "This is all there is..." And then we were born. We breathed our first breaths of air. We saw our mother. We saw light and the sky. We sucked our mother's breast. There was life after the womb. Then my brother died. I asked my mother, "Mother, do you think there is life after this life on earth?" And in my dream my mother answered, "No, this is all there is!" And then I woke up.

It is a beautiful dream.

But what do you make of it, Jesus?

Maybe your mother was wrong just like your brother was wrong. There was life after the womb. Maybe there is life after our time on earth. Anything is possible. What do you think?

Sometimes I think that maybe life is no different than a dream.

The old man's eyes were drooping. He went on. *You go to sleep, you wake up. You die, you wake up. But where, Jesus? Where do dead men wake up…? I can feel life being sucked out of me…I am being sucked into the tunnel of death…What is on the other side?*

Jesus answered calmly.

No one knows. But the most important thing is that you have lived. You have had this life. One must always appreciate the blessing of being alive.

Sometimes – when I have suffered or have watched others suffer – I have thought life is more of a curse than a blessing.

I can understand that thought. I have had it too. Do you sometimes wish you had died with your brother?

The old man hesitated.

Sometimes.

I suspect that at one time or another everyone thinks that life is not worth living. Even kings and princes. Maybe even God.

Yes…

But tell me, my dear friend…Have you ever felt great joy?

Yes…once …twice…a few times.

And didn't one moment of supreme joy make it all worthwhile?

That is possible Jesus…

As he said this, the old man's eyes closed. Jesus took his hand, bent forward, and kissed it. As he was about to set the hand back on the old man's chest, he felt it turning cold. He held it gently – between his two warm hands – as the old man's head fell to the side.

THIRTEEN

The woman did not need her anymore, so Mary came to live with Jesus.

FOURTEEN

The sunlight entered through the slits in the walls. Jesus rolled close to Mary and began licking her breast. With her hand, Mary slid the nipple into Jesus's mouth.

You are my son, my lover, and my father. You are all men to me. I never had a father and I have never had a son. I have had many lovers, but none like you. You will be my last lover, Jesus. You are the only lover I have ever loved.

Jesus moved his body, licked between the two breasts and began sucking the other one.

No man has made me feel like you make me feel. This night I dreamed you were my husband.

I am your husband, Jesus said. *We don't need the rabbis to pronounce us husband and wife. Why should they have the power to do that? Only you and I know how much we love each other. Only you and I can decide our marriage.*

In that case, we've been married since the first time we talked in the olive grove. Since that moment I have never wanted another man.

Nor I another woman.

Jesus's lips left Mary's breasts and found her face in the half light. His hands crawled across her body.

I didn't know I could feel this way about another human being.

I didn't either, Mary. I had never known what it was to truly love someone.

Do you think many people experience such a feeling?

I don't know, but I don't think so. I love every inch of your body and every thought in your head. I have never felt that way before about a woman.

Nor I about a man. How do such things happen?

Love is a mystery. Maybe a greater mystery than life.

When their bodies locked together they weren't making love…they were love.

Jesus and Mary discovered that you cannot truly make love unless you are truly in love. Sex was all over the earth. Love was in their bed.

FIFTEEN

For a while Jesus began working more. He built more chairs and tables. He built cupboards and beds. He had a friend named Peter who cut down trees and brought him long pieces of fine wood. Sometimes Mary helped Jesus with little details like making the wood smoother so that no slivers would find their way into people's skin. Otherwise she cooked and made the house comfortable.

In the evening before the sun disappeared they went for walks and talked about the world…

Does anyone know how big it is?

The Romans come from Rome. It takes months to walk from Rome.

Which way is it?

Jesus pointed in the direction of the sinking sun.

That way, I think, though I'm not sure.

Why do the Romans leave their homes to come here?

Why do birds fly from tree to tree? Maybe it is better here. Maybe their king wants to control the world.

Why would anyone want to control the world?

Why would anyone want to control anything? What is it in man that desires power…power over anything… over children, over animals, over a lover, over a population, over land…even over oneself? This is also a great mystery. From where does the urge to dominate come? Some creatures seek to dominate more than others. The Jewish god is said to have power over all of heaven and earth. Did He seek that power? The Roman gods fight each other for power. Perhaps man creates gods in his own image…hungry for domination and power. But it's interesting that the Jews don't try to conquer like the Romans. Maybe it's because the Jews have only the one God Almighty who already has all the power. The Roman gods continue their struggle for power; the Roman people continue to try to conquer.

The Romans want power on earth. The Jews want power in heaven.

I love your mind Mary.

Where did my mind come from?

It is so different from other minds.

Where does anything come from? It is you, Jesus, who has taught me to appreciate the mystery of all things. Now when I walk about the town, everything has become a matter of wonder – even plants and animals. I look at dogs. Some never bark; others bark incessantly. I observe plants. Some grow tall and spread and climb. Others stay small and take up little space.

It is the nature of nature.

The other day I watched a caterpillar climb up a wall. Where is it going? I wondered. Does it have a reason for going where it is going? What is pushing it onward? Then I asked the same questions as I watched the people of the village.

That is another great question. What is the motor behind all human actions? Behind all actions? Is there one great motor or are there many small motors?

They held each other's hand as they walked. The touch of fingers can be like making love.

The rabbis say God is the motor.

And if the god the rabbis talk about doesn't exist, then what is behind everything? And even if there is a god, what is the motor behind Him?

Jesus, I love how behind every question you see ten other questions.

Maybe it is better to ask no questions…or at least few questions.

That is what most people do.

And I think animals ask no questions. They just live…

And die.

And as they live and die they don't ask where they are going and where they came from. Only people ask these questions and they accept the first answers that are thrown in front of their faces. The Jews accept the answers the rabbis give. The Romans accept the answers their priests give.

And you Jesus, you accept no answers.

Jesus was quiet for a long moment. *The longer I live the closer I feel to the animals.*

But you just said animals don't ask questions.

Maybe animals don't ask questions because they know there are no answers.

Mary put her arm around Jesus's waist. He put his hand on her far shoulder. Both felt light as clouds.

I often wonder who or what is satisfied being what it is. Are people ever satisfied with who they are and what they have? Are animals satisfied? Are the moon and the sun happy being what they are? Are rocks and rivers and mountains?

Rivers go dry or overflow. Mountains explode or fall. Rocks crack and break.

Not all do.

We don't live long enough to know that.

Do you think that everything is always changing?

That is a thought that has often made me dizzy. So has the thought that the world cannot be stopped... that it is going where it's going and nothing can change its course.

Not even man?

Man is part of its course.

And God?

No one knows if there is a god. And even if God exists, maybe He is also just part of the course.

Jesus, does anyone else think like you do?

I don't know. I don't know anyone else who does. Maybe there are millions of people who think like me in some part of this world or in other worlds. Maybe there are thousands of worlds out there beyond the blue sky of day and the black sky of night. Maybe there are millions of creatures that think like me. I don't know. I don't even know where my thinking comes from. It just happens.

I love your thinking.

And I love yours, Mary. That is one thing I know.

Maybe the only question one can answer in this world is "Whom do I love?"

Maybe love is the only thing that has a core, a center, a heart. Maybe all the rest is in flux like the river and the wind.

Maybe love is the only thing that is eternal.

It might be eternal, but it is also the rarest of all diamonds.

Jesus and Mary stopped and kissed on the path where they were walking. Their bodies locked like pieces of an intricate puzzle. When their lips finally separated Jesus whispered:

I am getting hungry.

You are always hungry.

For you my darling.

I made a new kind of bread today. It has dried

grapes in it.
    Then let's go home and feast.

SIXTEEN

Here is what Jesus thought as he worked the following morning making a table for the Roman captain who knew that if he asked Jesus to make something it would get made.

When I'm near Mary, I feel as if my whole body is pulled toward hers. It is as if I am inside her and she is inside me. Is it possible that two humans can actually blend together, melt together, truly experience "living" together? I had always felt so alone in this world. Of course, I am friendly with all the people I meet – at least I try to be as I never want to make life worse for any creature – but until I met Mary, I had never had anybody I could share and exchange everything with. It is as if our guts and brains have been mixed together and have been put into one body...love's body... Sometimes Mary gets worried and thinks I don't love her and that I care about other women. Sometimes I even think the same about her. But such feelings never last. We both know that there is no other person on earth that we can love the way we love each other…I am fascinated by everything in the world, but I am most fascinated by the feeling I have for Mary. When we are together – walking, sitting at the table, in bed, anywhere – I feel her presence as if she were a bonfire that constantly heats every part of my body. It is as if through Mary the whole world has become a warm and beautiful place instead of a cold ugly place…What is the world in itself? Nothing. It is only what we make of it. It is only the human head that decides what it is… And as every human is different, every vision of the world is different…With Mary, my vision has changed. Things that used to have no meaning are now charged with meaning…a bird, a cloud, the wind, a piece of bread, the tiniest insect…everything is fascinating and mysterious…The explosion of love is an explosion of life…And death? What is death in all this? If life cannot be eternal, love must be eternal. Love must conquer death. If there is no God, one must become God. Tragedy would be if death brought an end to our love…I cannot imagine our love ending. I cannot imagine the world ending. The Jews see death as opening the door to heaven. For them death is not tragic. But does death open anything except a hole in the ground wherein a body is dropped and covered to be eaten by worms? All I know is that this life is precious. It's all we have, like the man who only has one donkey. That donkey becomes everything…Does life only regenerate on earth? New trees grow. New babies get born…But are the dead dead forever…? All I know is that since I have known Mary, the world has become a diamond, a jewel floating somewhere in the middle of everywhere…of nowhere…

Jesus worked on the table until the sun disappeared for the day. He had promised the Roman captain it would be ready for Saturday, a *feriae imperativae* – a day of celebration. The Romans had many holidays. Sometimes even the slaves were given time to rest. But such things depended on the emperors; some had bigger hearts than others. The emperors were the gods on earth. They could often be cruel.

SEVENTEEN

The Roman captain was a most pleasant person. His name was Marcus. When he came with three of his men to pick up the table, Jesus had them sit down at it and offered them all a glass of wine. The soldiers were young, not more than eighteen, but they listened as their boss and Jesus talked.

You have done fine work on the table Jesus. It's good to have a carpenter I can count on.

It's good to have a Roman captain who pays. A few minutes before, the captain had slipped three denarius coins into Jesus's hand.

You've had bad experiences in the past?

A few times. Not just with Romans, but also with Jews and Greeks.

There are good and bad people everywhere.

You would know more than I. I have never travelled

far from my home. Tell me Marcus, what are the people like in Rome?

Most are very pleasant, but much depends on the circumstances of their lives. Much, but not everything. There are gentle rich people and there are cruel rich people. Most of the poor are meek, but there are poor people who can murder.

I have spent half of my life trying to figure out why some people are kind and others are cruel.

Have you found an answer?

No, but the more I think about it, the more I believe a human being has no more free will than a dog. Some dogs are kind, others are cruel. Why? Dogs don't "choose" to be kind? They don't "choose" to be cruel. No one would say that. They just turn out the way they are for an infinity of reasons. I think the same is true for men. One cannot blame a man for being a fool. One can only blame the world. One should not praise a man for being kind. One should praise the world.

And that is why you don't judge people?

Yes. No one truly knows another person's life. Without knowledge one has no right to judge. And knowledge is never complete. Others have no right to judge me, so I don't judge them. No one knows my life and I know no one else's life.

I agree with you, Jesus.

Friends tend to think alike.

What fascinates me is how some people always have power over others. And whoever has power judges and decides what is right and wrong, good and bad. Power always thinks it has the right answers.

You're a wise Roman captain, Marcus. Have some more wine.

Thank you.

And your men, too.

They are barely men, but they serve me well.

They must drink.

And I must ask you a question. I have heard it said that you, Jesus of Nazareth, think that you are a god. Is that true?

Jesus laughed. That is a perfect example of how stupid people are. I don't blame them for their stupidity, but that doesn't take it away...Marcus, nothing is farther from the truth. It is true that I don't believe in the Jewish god or the Roman gods. I see no proof for any gods. I look at the world and have no idea where it came from, where it's headed or why we are here. When I say "we", I mean everything – animals, plants, rocks, the sun, the moon. It is also true that I have said that if there is no God, man must become God. But that is a play on words. I have no idea what a "god" might be. I think all the gods I have heard about are simply inventions of the human mind. A "real" god might be something totally different, something that no man could possibly understand. When I say man must become God, all I mean is that man must try to become better. He must try to be less stupid, less cruel, less flat-headed...less of what I see him to be today. But of course, maybe that's impossible. Maybe man can never be other than what he is.

Do you prefer the Jewish god or the Roman gods?

The young soldiers drank their wine and looked intently at Jesus. They had never heard such a conversation before.

I have no preference. I think both are rather odd. The Jewish god can be cruel and seems to seek constant adoration. Tell me, Marcus, why would a god want people to pray to him constantly? Why would a god want to be "worshipped"? Men who want to be worshipped look silly to me. They are weak. They are unsure of themselves. A strong man does not need other people to tell him he is such.

And the Roman gods? Do you like them better than the Jewish god?

They are droll. They are just like people. They play and fight and love and hate. They get offended and they seek revenge. They are not "god-like" …they are "people-like."

And so what would a god be like, Jesus?

I have no idea Marcus. None. Zero. That is part of the great mystery of existence. But I just look at the suffering, death, and the horrors of the world and wonder why.

Why what?

Why wars are fought…why people get sick and die…why criminals steal and kill…why women are raped…why people are nailed to wooden crosses and left to die…why children are whipped…Sometimes I think man is the worst animal on earth. Only men kill each other without the intention of eating. Animals don't do this. They only kill to eat…to survive. Men kill animals to eat and they kill each other because they are stupid. I often think the words "man" and "animal" are very wrong and misunderstood. Often man is more "animal" than the animals and animals are more "man" than men.

You're right Jesus. I myself often look at birds and think they are the greatest creatures on earth. No man can fly through the sky.

Yes Marcus. Birds are so beautiful and skilled.

Have you ever seen a lion or a tiger?

No, but I have heard about them.

They too are amazing. Like horses, they can run much faster than men. They can kill a man with great ease.

But do they kill for stupid reasons?

They only kill when they are hungry or feel endangered.

Men kill men for land and power and foolish ideas about justice and religion.

And that is why you say man must try to become God?

That is why I say man must try to become better than he is.

But can he?

I have my doubts. We can only try.

Who is "we", Jesus?

You...me...anybody who thinks like we do.

Most men don't think like we do.

Most men don't think; they follow.

There was a silence around the table now in Jesus's house. Jesus poured more wine for everybody. Finally Marcus spoke again.

I think we must be going Jesus. We must prepare things for tomorrow's festival.

Every day should be a festival...even days when we work. From birth to death life should be a celebration.

Thank you for the table.

It's my pleasure to work for you.

Before leaving the captain added: *I see a woman's robe over there on the bed. Do you have a wife now, Jesus?*

I have a woman, not a wife. And I love her more than anything on earth.

You are very lucky Jesus.

We are very lucky.

The Romans picked up the table and were gone.

EIGHTEEN

Mary kissed Jesus and then stared at the ceiling. They had been locked together in love for half an hour and now were resting. Jesus looked at Mary's face.

Mary, if there is a god in heaven who decides to judge me positively when I die and says to me, 'Jesus, what I liked about you was that you were an honest man and tried to be good to other creatures. Even though you doubted me, I am still going to let you stay with me in heaven. Had I been in your place, I probably would have doubted me too…So, I have decided to let you draw the woman you want to spend eternity with. Show me exactly the woman you want and I will create her for you…Mary, I would draw you. Exactly as I see you now. Everything. Your eyes, nose, mouth, arms, legs, breasts, shoulders, hair, teeth, feet, hands…exactly like you are. That is how much I love you. And then if God said, 'Tell me what kind of brain you want in the head of this woman,' I would tell him about your brain and I would have it all too. That is how much I love you.

And Mary was filled with joy and she said to Jesus, *And I will say the same thing to God about you.*

Jesus's right eye became teary and soon they were locked again together in love. If there is an all-seeing eternal God, He looked down on them and witnessed what true love is, the fusion of two bodies into one. No separation. No me here and you there. If it didn't happen with Adam and Eve, it was happening with Jesus and Mary.

And when they finally unlocked and lay side by side on the bed of straw, Mary said, *I know what heaven feels like.*

What? Jesus asked.

Orgasm.

They both laughed and wondered if it could possibly be true.

Darkness was coming to the world. Mary rose from the bed and went outside to pee. Jesus prepared the table with plates, bread, olives, and wine. Mary returned and they supped in candlelight.

They slept until the sun returned, waking only once for Jesus to pee before returning them both to Mary's idea of paradise.

NINETEEN

Mary had risen early and gone to the market. Love had flown her through the night and when she walked she felt like her arms were the wings of an angel. She didn't know life could feel so good. She didn't walk; she danced. She didn't think; her mind was a flowerbed. She didn't go to the market alone; Jesus was in her soul…

Speaking of souls, Jesus lay in bed wondering what a soul might be. People talked about souls and bodies as if one was as real as the other. His body he could touch. He lived inside of it. He was it. But his soul? What was that? Maybe he did not live inside his body. Maybe he was only body. Then he wondered about his thoughts…all people's thoughts…Where do they come from? Do they come from the mind or are they the mind? Is the mind the soul? When the Jews pray to God are they really just praying to their own minds? Are their souls simply talking to themselves? Is thinking a bodily process like peeing? Is peeing a spiritual process like thinking? Are spirit and soul the same thing? Or are they the same no thing…the same nothing? The priests talk about the spirit of man and the spirit of God as if they were as tangible as bread and olives. But what are they…? Really?

Then Jesus wondered where the world came from. He had learned the word "cosmology" when he was a boy. It came from the Greeks who liked to think about the cosmos. Jesus couldn't help thinking about the cosmos. He couldn't help thinking about the biggest things and the smallest things. He couldn't help thinking about causality, about what caused what. Did God cause everything? What caused God? The Jews had their answers. The Romans had their answers. The Greeks had other answers, similar to the Roman answers and very different from the Jews. That allowed for only three possibilities. Maybe there were others. Maybe there were other parts of the earth where people had very different ideas about where everything came from and where everything was going…

Jesus couldn't help being Jesus. He couldn't help being inquisitive. He couldn't accept simple answers to the most profound questions. Sometimes he wondered if maybe there were no answers to the profound questions. The more Jesus thought about things, the less he knew about things. The priests had simple answers for everything. They took the answers that their fathers had taken and their fathers' fathers had taken. The Romans did the same. The Greeks did the same. Jesus could not be satisfied with his fathers' answers.

Sometimes when he thought these kinds of thoughts, Jesus was full of fear and trembling. Sometimes his head would feel like it was going to explode, and he would feel so alone. But this morning when he thought these thoughts of cosmology, he felt no fear and his body didn't tremble once. Why? Because he had just spent the most beautiful night with Mary. And the day with Mary had been beautiful. And the day and the night before had been beautiful… Since he had met Mary, his feeling about everything had changed. Where there had been darkness, now there was light. Where there had been fear, now there was comfort. Where there had been ugliness, now there was beauty. Where there had been hate, now there was love. Where there had been death, now there was life…

With these thoughts in his mind, Jesus began to think about how some people (and animals too – for Jesus was a lover of birds and four-legged creatures and even creatures with no legs) could be in such horrible situations and others could be in such wonderful situations…people in the same world, in the same town, even in the same family. A woman here could be so happy and in such good health. A woman there could be so sad and sick and suffering. How? Why? Who or what was to blame? Was the person to blame? Was the world to blame? Was life to blame? Was God to blame? And what if nothing was to blame? Or everything?

Here as Jesus lay in bed with the smell of Mary on his fingers, he had a thought that very few men have, a thought that would color his life forever: What if everything that existed was totally innocent? What if nothing that existed was responsible for being what it was? What if everything in all cosmology was not "caused", but just "was"? Or what if all causes were tied together and could not be separated? Didn't both amount to the same thing...? That nothing was to blame...Or everything was to blame...but then "blame" was the wrong word. A better word would be "responsible" ...everything was responsible for everything else...But that was not true either...No, nothing was responsible. Everything just was. Everything was like a newborn baby. No baby asked to be born. No baby asked to have the parents it had. No tree asked to be planted. No cloud asked to float through the sky. No sun asked to burn in the sky. The sky didn't ask to hold the planets. The planets and moon didn't ask to turn around the earth. Maybe the earth was turning around something it didn't choose too...

Jesus's thoughts then flew from the biggest things to the smallest things...but his ideas were the same.

Nothing asked to be what it was. Everything was innocent.

These thoughts might have felt different if he hadn't been so in love with Mary.

TWENTY

Who was Herod? Much has been said and written about him, but did anyone have access to the depths of his heart and head and urinary tract? Did he ever love anyone? Did anyone ever love him? It is said he had eleven wives. Were they all forced to marry him? Did any marry for love? Did all marry with an eye on wealth and power? Does anyone know the secrets of his wives' lives? Why does anybody end up marrying anybody else? What infinity of circumstances brings any two people together? How could Herod build such a beautiful temple when he was such a bad man who would kill his own wives and children? What made Herod be Herod? Even Herod didn't know.

What motor propels one man to kill, conquer, and enslave and another man to wander in the desert and contemplate the beauty of a flower? One generation produces Herod. The next produces Jesus.

The Jews say they are children of God. Whose god? Which god? Did God not want women to read and write? Maybe that was not such a bad thing, for what would women have been reading? The Bible? An eyeful of lies about the history of the world?

What can be said of a world full of so many slaves? What can be said of a world filled with so much suffering? What can be said of a world with something so beautiful as the love between Mary and Jesus?

The Jews say the flesh of a pig is unclean and should never be eaten. It is their law. Whence cometh this law? Probably from a man who got sick after eating part of a pig a few thousand years ago. The man called himself a prophet. He was full of bad pig and full of dumb shit. But his law has lasted for more than two millennia.

From where do ideas about right and wrong come? Why are the world's laws what they are? What is the origin of good and evil? Are Mary and Jesus committing adultery? Are they sinning? Are they committing love? Are they writing a new Bible?

Aren't all of "God's laws" really just "man's laws?" And aren't they usually conceived of by unhappy men who take their unhappiness out on other people? Don't they simply want others to share their misery? Isn't it because their bodies are sick that they denigrate the flesh? Do they not want others to feel guilty so they can pull them into their mud? Aren't they keen to enslave the minds and flesh of others because they themselves are not strong enough to be free?

For years Jesus listened to the rabbis talk. When he asked such questions they had no answers. Or if they did have answers, they were bad answers. Dead answers. Answers that were not real. Answers with no foundation. They would say things like, "Because it is written in the Torah." And then Jesus would ask, "But why is what is written in the Torah true?" And they would say, "Because it is the Word of God." And Jesus would ask, "But how do you know it is the Word of God? The Romans and Greeks have different gods. Which god or gods are real? No one has seen God. No one has talked to God. No one really knows anything about God." And when Jesus would say this, the rabbis always looked at him like he was crazy, muttered among themselves about Moses and burning bushes, but without conviction. But he was quite sure that he wasn't the one who was crazy.

The rabbis had no idea why they believed what they believed. Didn't they believe what they believed because their fathers had believed it? Weren't their beliefs based on one thing and one thing only: tradition? They would never answer yes to these questions because to do so would leave them naked, lonely, lost, afraid. They, like most men, were not strong enough to create new values and new reasons to live. So they followed their fathers who had followed their fathers' fathers.

Jesus did not think all this was necessarily bad. He simply thought it was human. Humans were weak. Even Herod was at bottom weak. Doesn't one who kills his wives and sons do so because he himself is weak?

The Bible of the Jews says, "Thou shalt not kill." But the Bible doesn't mean that thou shalt never kill. It means, "Thou shalt not kill except when God tells thee to kill," which historically was quite often. God tells thee to kill when people are "wicked" and don't believe in Him...

So Jesus would say to the rabbis, "But if people have different gods and these different gods all say that it is okay to kill people who don't believe in their god, then we have war. Isn't war bad?" And the rabbis would say that there was only one true god and that true god was their God. And Jesus would point out that the other side thought their god was the true god. But the rabbis would dismiss him as a fool or a troublemaker...

So Jesus began to think that it was all a circus. But whose fault was it? Was it a man's fault if he was too weak to believe in anything except the traditions of his fathers? Was it a man's fault if he was jealous or stupid? People can't help themselves. People can't be other than what they are. People don't understand who they are and why they do what they do.

Jesus thought about these things. He eventually stopped talking to the rabbis.

Seasons passed. Years passed "Can one know the truth?" Jesus began to wonder. "Probably not," he thought. "But maybe one can know what the lies are."

Jesus tried diligently to respect other people and their beliefs. But if these other people didn't respect each other or didn't respect him, then what was he to do? If these others said that he and Mary were adulterous sinners and wanted to kill Mary, then what should he do? Stand and watch? If they wanted to kill him, what should he do? Let them? Jesus wouldn't blame them because he knew that they could be nothing other than what they were. "Blame" was not part of Jesus's vocabulary. But were there not limits to what one could tolerate?

Little by little Jesus began to see life as a kind of jungle, as a savage place. He saw that the only thing that ruled the world was power. Herod had had power. Now his son had power. Pontius Pilate had power. Some of the rabbis had power. Power moved from one person to another, from one group to another. Laws were made by those who had power. Slaves had no power. Women had no power. They never said who should do what. They never made the rules.

Jesus wondered what was good and what was bad. He realized that what was good for one was often bad for another. What was good for the Romans was bad for the Jews and vice versa. Perhaps the world was not a moral place. Could it be made better? Could the slaves be freed? Could women one day share the power? Would there ever be "goodness" and "truth" on earth?

Jesus did not know. But of one thing he was quite certain: all the talk he had heard about heaven and hell and another world after death was probably a pack of lies. He had never seen any dead man come back to life. Never...Did that mean there was nothing after death and nothing before birth? Of course, he didn't know. No one knew. But he and everyone else did know that there was a here and a now. Why did people ignore this life and talk about an "afterlife?" This was the real sin. The Kingdom of God – if there was one – was here and now. It had to be. That was the only thing that made sense. This life must be cherished. This life must be loved and respected. The odds were that this life was all there was...

Thus thought Jesus one summer day in the part of the world called Palestine.

TWENTY-ONE

When Mary and Jesus made love together they were both amazed that the feeling was so different from when they had made love with other people before. With others Jesus had never felt like he could make love forever. With others Mary had never felt her flesh heat up until it eventually melted into the other's body. With each other, Mary and Jesus became one. Each totally loved the other. They loved the self. The self became the other. The other became the self.

When this kind of feeling is present you cease to make love; you become love. There's no geometry or mathematical calculation because there's no separation. There aren't two bodies interacting because there's only one body loving. There's no you and I; there's only we.

Jesus and Mary wondered how many people in the

world had a chance to feel the way they felt. They imagined very few. An infinity of circumstances had been necessary to bring them together. It would take another infinity to pull them apart.

TWENTY-TWO

How often is a human being able to climb out of his or her box? Here of course we're talking about the mental box...the box of thinking, language, values, beliefs... The Greeks and Romans thought many things about cosmology. They often did not agree with each other. Parmenides, Anaxagoras, Epicurus, Aristotle, Ptolemy, Empedocles, Plutarch, Zeno, Cicero, and many others had ideas about where everything came from, what it was made of, and how it worked. There was little consensus. Jewish cosmology was monolithic. Everyone agreed. The Jews stapled themselves to the Biblical cosmology which seems to have been based on old Babylonian ideas: the Earth and the Heavens form a unit within the "infinite waters of chaos" ...the earth is flat and circular and a solid dome – "the firmament" – keeps out the chaos. And, of course, there was the story of one God, Jehovah, creating everything in six days, then taking a much-deserved rest. Eventually Christianity and Islam bought into the Jewish cosmology and pounded it into the head of the Western world until Copernicus and Galileo came along. But they were forced to shut up and it took a few more centuries before any real climbing out of the Jewish-Christian-Islamic box was possible. And only a small group of people were able to do it. Most people's minds are still today deeply colored by the old Jewish vision of God creating the world, man being "free," and hell waiting to suck up the sinners after death and heaven opening its doors to the good.

Take a few minutes one clear summer day and lie on your back in a field or on a park bench and look at the sky. I don't say look "up" at the sky because the odds are there is no "up" or "down" in the universe. When you look at the sky imagine all the explanations we have for everything. But there is an immediate problem: we don't really have any idea what "everything" is. Sure, we have our box of 21st century science and the universe being around for 13,000,000,000 years and the "big-bang" and all that. But isn't that too a residue of the old Babylonian idea of "a creation" and time being linear. What about the mystery, the great mystery of it all? And just imagine, as hard as it tries and as profound as it thinks itself to be, maybe the human mind can never really know...

If you look at the sky long enough and let your mind

fly far enough and put all preconceived ideas in parentheses, you will eventually start to get dizzy. The deep deep mystery will hit you. All cosmologies will look feeble, like paltry endeavors of the human head to explain things. When you finally stand up again, if you are weak you will depart with heavy feet and go bury yourself in the nearest safe dark cave…say a newspaper, or a TV, or a church. If you are strong you will dance toward nowhere with light feet, your head high, and your nose pointed toward the sun.

TWENTY-THREE

When Jesus finally stood up he felt light-headed. He didn't know how long he had been lying in the grass on the hill in the olive grove. No watches or clocks in the Holy Land. Only the sun and shadows to tell the time and because sun was fat and low, he imagined Mary would be waiting for him.

She was.

Where did you go?

I went up to the olive grove where we first walked together. I lay down and looked at the sky.

And what did you see?

Your face on a big blue wall. But first I thought about everything I could think about.

You think too much Jesus.

Do you think so my darling?

Where can all this thinking take you? It is always a

dead end.

Maybe so, but let me tell you what I thought.

Of course. If nothing else, I love the sound of your voice.

And I love yours…I thought about all the things that I've been told my whole life through. I thought about what my parents told me and what the rabbis tried to drill into my head. I thought about what my Roman friend Marcus told me about how the Romans see the world. I thought about what my friends John, Paul, Matthew and Mark think about everything. And then I stared at the blue sky and wondered if it was a ceiling like the Jews say or an infinity like some of the Greeks and Romans say.

And which did you vote for?

I didn't vote. I tried to think of other possibilities.

That is so you, Jesus. Mary laughed, but lovingly so. *You always see the complexity of everything.*

I can see nothing else. Things are deep. Time is deep. Space is deep. Every tree, flower, donkey, and man is deep. But the human mind is shallow. Too readily satisfied with simple answers, answers like the rabbis give.

Yes, if there is one thing I have learned from you, Jesus, it is that.

And what is the deepest thing of all, my love?

I've learned that too. But only because I feel it, not because I think it.

Feeling is everything.

And that is why love is the deepest thing of all. It is love that is felt the deepest.

And that is why when I looked at the sky, I saw your face. I see you everywhere. I feel you everywhere.

And what is felt the deepest is also perhaps the greatest mystery.

Everything is a mystery.

Not to shallow minds.

To shallow minds everything can be explained.

Why would anyone want to explain the feeling I have for you?

I don't know, Jesus said.

Mary and Jesus moved closer and closer to each other. And Jesus moved closer to an absurd crucifixion.

TWENTY-FOUR

Good morning Marcus.

Good morning Jesus.

What are you doing here so early?

I want to talk to you, to warn you.

To warn me about what? Is war approaching? Someone invading?

No, it's secure. We have almost all the world under our control.

Exactly how big is the world?

We don't know for sure. We haven't seen it all. No one has walked and walked without eventually turning back.

I have walked for three days in every direction. That is what I have seen.

And I have ridden a horse for a hundred days to get here. That is what I have seen.

So what is it you want to warn me about, Marcus my friend?

People are talking about you Jesus. Both Romans and Jews. Some of my officers are saying you are beginning to disturb the peace in Palestine. And the rabbis say you are blaspheming God.

How can I be disturbing the peace when I have never injured a man or an animal in my life?

They fear you might incite a revolt.

A revolt? Against whom?

Us. The Romans. Pontius Pilate.

I'm not stupid. Someone will always have power. Your lot aren't bad people. Better Romans have the power than some other crueler people.

I know that's what you think, but they don't.

Well, tell them.

I have no power. They won't listen to me. I'm a lowly captain. Only twenty men under my command.

If you don't want to tell them, I will. I have nothing to hide.

They might come and talk to you soon Jesus. That is what I've heard. They want to hear your ideas firsthand.

Marcus, the only revolt that interests me is the revolt of a man against himself. One cannot change the world, but one can change oneself.

But maybe you can change the world, Jesus. You have something about you that makes people listen to you.

People might listen, but they don't hear. There are very few people I have talked to who understand me. Even my friends Paul, Mark, John, and Matthew misinterpret what I say.

What do you mean?

They think I am the son of God. Every man is the son of God and every woman is the daughter of God. But those words mean nothing because no one knows who God is or what God might be. We are all really sons and daughters of the earth. But so are donkeys, goats, sheep, serpents, flowers, trees and clouds. My friends cannot escape the idea of the Jewish god. They want me to pretend I am the awaited son. I make no such pretension. No one knows where the earth came from.

If you had been born in Rome, maybe people would have said you were the son of Jupiter.

I don't know. We will never know because I was born here in Bethlehem. A man lives his life only once. All he can try to do is make the best of it…and try to help others have a chance to have a good life along the way.

A good life being…?

Marcus, each man must search his own heart and find his own way. Most men don't search very hard. They simply accept the world and beliefs they are born into. Very few men think for themselves. Very few men wonder and marvel and look behind the surface at the great complexity and mystery of life.

Maybe men are afraid of the mystery and complexity.

Yes, either afraid or incapable of seeing it.

Then it's not their fault.

That's true Marcus. But like water makes a flower grow, I hope my words will make people grow. But there's no guarantee. The majority of men are like sheep. They follow the herd. This isn't so much a bad thing. It's just a necessary thing. And, if a man is a sheep then let him have his Shepherd. If he must blindly follow the herd, then so be it.

And you have nothing against the herd, Jesus?

Most people are stuck in the world they are born into, like trees planted in the ground. If the herd followed me in a revolt, they'd still be a herd. When the revolt was over they'd still be sheep. So I'm not interested in followers. Of course, I love all mankind like I love all of the night sky. But I love most the star that shines in the night. I want to see men flying with their own wings. I want to see men take their own road. I want each man to find his own heaven on earth.

And what might that heaven be, Jesus?

I can't tell you. You must find it for yourself. I'm not you. I can't prescribe what's good for you. You must discover that yourself. That is why I want no followers. Followers will always be weak. I want to see people grow strong.

You are wise Jesus. You must tell all this to the Roman leaders. They fear you want power over the people.

I want power only over myself. If your leaders come, I will tell them what I think. I will tell them what a great mystery this world is.

For them, life is not a mystery. They only care about their stomachs and their penises.

They are human. I often think I should never expect more of a man than that he cares about his stomach and his penis. One cannot make wine out of water. One cannot make a snail fly. But I can't help trying, Marcus. I can't help dreaming of a heaven on earth.

No. But you must also take care Jesus. People are misunderstanding your ideas. And power hates to be questioned.

You're quite right. If and when your leaders come, I'll be careful. But I'll be honest. I mean no harm to Roman or Jew.

I'll be going now Jesus. My men are waiting. We're making a road from Nazareth to Bethlehem.

Thank you for coming by Marcus. Goodbye my dear friend.

Goodbye, Jesus.

TWENTY-FIVE

When Jesus and Mary made love that night, he thought he was going to disappear into her belly. Not the first time, but the second. The first time he was as strong as a wild bull and he roared as he sent his thick juice into her heart. But the second time, perhaps a half an hour later, he felt like a delicate little mouse scurrying into the hole of its mother and when his juice flew he whimpered softly and flew with it and dissolved in the womb from which he came.

TWENTY-SIX

The next morning Jesus went looking for his friends, John, Mark, Matthew and Paul. He had known them for many years and they had shared many moments together. Like all friends, sometimes they spent more time together than others. Since Jesus had met Mary, he saw them less.

They were sitting in a shady area in Nazareth's central square.

Where have you been Jesus? Has Mary put a leash around your neck? Have you become a dog?

I have nothing against dogs. Sometimes I think it would be better to be a dog than a man. At least some dogs run free.

Ha! You've said many times that nothing is free.

You're right, John. I have no idea what freedom might be. Maybe a dog on a leash can be freer than a dog running in the wild.

Would you rather be a dog or a donkey, a Roman or a Jew, a man or a woman, a God or a sun?

I would be happy to be any and all of them. Just existing is the greatest gift.

Are you crazy Jesus or are you the son of God, like Paul reckons you say you are?

I never said he was the son of God, John. What I said was that if there was a son of God in Palestine it was Jesus. But I never said there was a son of God in Palestine.

And I would never say I am the son of God, Jesus rejoined, because I have no idea if there is a god. There is no proof of any deity.

The rabbis say we don't need proof; we only need faith.

I know Mark. We heard the rabbis say this a thousand times. But tell me why I should direct my faith in the direction of the Jewish god instead of the Roman gods…or any other god for that matter.

You directed your faith toward Mary…

Mary is real. She walks and talks.

She has a spirit…God is spirit…

What does "spirit" mean? You don't know. I don't know. The rabbis don't know. No one knows.

Why do you doubt everything Jesus?

Because when I was a boy the rabbis said I must seek the truth. I did. And the truth became very complicated. The more I thought, the less truth became evident. Maybe there is no truth.

Do you think the Bible is a lie?

The rabbis just wanted me to believe "their" truth. I have no idea what is true. But I have no proof that the Bible is any truer than the Roman version of the world.

Maybe we should start a religion based on lies.

Maybe all religions are based on lies. Why should we start another one?

Maybe we can start a better world.

The only thing that can make the world better is love.

Then let us start a religion based on love.

Love can only happen between two people. As soon as more than two people are involved, love falls apart. There will never be a religion based on love. Love is a private matter.

The Bible says "Love thy neighbor as thyself."

That is not a good commandment. Most people do not love themselves. The Bible says "Do unto others as you would have them do unto you." This too is a bad idea because most people do not treat themselves well. If you don't know how to treat yourself, how can you expect to know how to treat others?

What are you saying Jesus? That there are no good commandments?

I don't know. But things are more complicated than the rabbis and the Bible make them out to be. For me, the only thing that counts is that every man finds his own road to heaven. And heaven must be here on earth. And at the end of that road there is probably love.

So you and Mary are in heaven?

Yes. And you can be too. All men can.

All men aren't as lucky as you are Jesus.

All I know is that others cannot make heaven for you. You must make it yourself. And when you make it with someone you love, it is even better.

So a slave can live a heavenly life…

Yes, if the slave finds love.

And a king can live a life in hell…

Yes, if he never finds love. Look at Herod. He had eleven wives and power over all of Palestine, yet his life was hell. No one ever loved him and he never truly loved anyone. Love is the only religion that makes any sense. And any church with more than two people is too big. People who love, see the world as a heaven. People who never love see the world as a hell. It is that simple.

But what about heaven and hell in the next world?

Paul, I have never seen the next world. Neither have you. Neither has any rabbi.

But some have had visions.

The kingdom of God is here and now. It is all we know. All men can enter the kingdom. There is no need for a judgment. No man can judge another man.

It is God's job to judge.

And if there is no God?

If there is no God, then the only judges are men.

And men are always bad judges. Men never truly understand the world. They never understand what causes what. When men judge they simply eliminate what they don't like. They punish what they don't agree with. That is not judgment; that is simply the exercising of power.

So what should one do?

Find your own way. Love. Marvel at the mystery of everything around you.

But what if there is no love on my road? What if everything around me is ugly, cruel, and stupid?

Then life is hell and tragic. To climb out of hell a man must be very strong. Only a great man can build a new road.

The friends were silent for a while. John had the pitcher of wine. He offered a cup to Jesus, then he filled his other friends' glasses. They drank together, each in his own thoughts.

TWENTY-SEVEN

When he was ten, Jesus had helped his father build the door to their house. It was the first real work he had ever done and his father had made him feel proud. When the two Roman soldiers pounded on that door, Jesus knew who was on the other side and why they were there.

Would you like to come in and share some bread and wine?

We have no time for bread and wine. Are you Jesus of Nazareth?

I am called that.

Then you must come with us to see Pontius Pilate.

Why does he want to see me?

That is not our business. He told us to fetch you immediately. We follow his orders.

I have been very lucky in my life. I have had to

follow very few orders. Do you enjoy following the orders of others?

That is not a question we ask ourselves.

Maybe you should.

We are soldiers. Soldiers do what they are told.

That is a strange way to live.

You must come with us.

If I must, I must. But I would rather eat bread and drink wine with you and talk about the mystery of life. Do you feel the wonderful mystery of being alive?

What mystery? We are Roman soldiers. We were born in Rome. We were sent here. We follow the orders of Pontius Pilate.

And one day you will die. And what will you have done with your lives?

We will have been soldiers and will have served the emperor.

Yes. It is a strange world we live in where everybody serves somebody else.

Jesus, you seem to be a kind man, but we really must not linger.

Will I be away long? Mary will worry if so.

That is not our business.

I am sure it isn't.

It was a quite a long walk to the palace where Pontius Pilate ruled. Jesus asked the soldiers many questions. They asked Jesus none.

There were two guards at the entrance. When the

trio arrived the doors were opened. Jesus was happy to get out of the heat of day and into a cool building. He was taken to Pontius Pilate's private office. The soldiers stood at the back of the room while Jesus and the ruler talked.

Good morning Jesus of Nazareth. I've been wanting to meet you.

And I wanted to meet you too Pilate.

Please be seated and let's discuss. We'll waste no time with petty talk…My first question is, who do you think you are Jesus?

That is a wonderful question. One of the most wonderful questions a man could be asked.

So answer it.

I can't.

Why not?

Because no man knows who he is. We think we know who we are. We have a name and a place of birth, a family, a language, a religion, a political system. But that tells us nothing about how our minds' and bodies' function. That tells us nothing about the why and wherefore of our beating hearts, the blood in our veins, and the stream of thoughts blowing through our brains.

It is the thoughts that I'm interested in. Do you think that you are the son of God?

If I thought I was the son of God, which god would I be the son of…the Jewish god Jehovah or one of your many Roman gods?

You're a Jew. You would think yourself to be the son of Jehovah.

You say I'm a Jew because I was born a Jew. But in my head I'm not a Jew. I don't believe in the god Jehovah any more than I believe in the god Jupiter or any other of your Roman gods.

But you believe in a Creator of the world?

I have no idea where the world came from. And no one else does either. You Romans have your explanation. The Jews have their explanation. The Greeks have theirs. Why should I believe one explanation over another? I have no proof or reason to believe in a God. For me the world is a great mystery.

Then you do not think you are the son of God?

No.

Do you think you are God?

That is a totally different question.

Why?

Because if there is no God to follow, who should one follow? Should one follow another man or should one follow oneself? That becomes the question. Should you be my god, Pilate? Should a rabbi be my god? Should a philosopher like Aristotle or Heraclitus be my god? Or should I be my own god?

I can see that you have talked with many philosophers.

No, not really. Mostly I've thought for myself. I've observed people and the world and tried to understand the world. I've tried to think about my thinking and the thinking of others.

Thinking can be dangerous, Jesus of Nazareth.

Dangerous to whom?

To you, to me, to everybody.

It is "not thinking" that's dangerous. People accept silly versions of what life is. They accept silly versions of what good and evil are. They accept silly versions of how they should live, how they should spend their time on earth. Look at all the slaves in the world. Look at your soldiers. They have no life. Their lives are worse than the lives of most dogs or donkeys.

We treat our soldiers very well. They're well fed. We keep them warm in winter.

Yes, but they're slaves to you. They spend their lives following orders. They never think for themselves. They don't possess their own lives. You possess their lives. The only thing they do on their own is rape the women of Palestine.

Don't presume…

Isn't all we think some sort of presumption?

Pontius Pilate said nothing, but Jesus went on.

And look at the lives of most women in this world. The Jews don't let their women read and write. Women have no power. They're slaves to men. They're forced to make love even if they don't want to, not only to your soldiers, but to their husbands. Can you imagine being forced to make love, Pilate, to a woman you didn't like…even hated? Can you imagine that?

I'm asking the questions.

I thought we were having a discussion.

You're a strong man, Jesus. Strong men are dangerous.

To whom? You're a strong man too, Pilate. Are you dangerous…? No, because you have the power. You only see me as dangerous because I might be a threat to it. But I threaten nobody's power. I want power only over myself.

Admit that's a lie, Jesus! Surely you want men to be free?

I fear men will never be free. Only animals are free…free until they are killed by other animals or trapped and killed or enslaved by men. Man himself was only ever free if and when he was an animal.

You believe that? You believe that man might have once been an animal?

The truth is, I think man has always been an animal…only now he is a different kind of animal. Now he is an enslaved animal. It's possible that he used to be wild, like goats on a mountain, like hawks in the sky. Maybe he used to run free, his eyes only looking out. But now he lives in society. Society enslaves him. Society tells him who he is and how he must act. Society tells him if he is good or evil. The Jews think the Jews good and the Romans evil. The Romans think the Romans good and the Jews evil. Society makes man silly and weak. Society judges man and makes him feel guilty.

Would you prefer a society with no laws, Jesus?

Of course, man must have some laws. But laws should exist only to help man live the best life possible, to make him strong, to make him maximize his time on earth.

And who should decide what the good life is?

That is the question, Pontius Pilate...Who should decide? You? Me? The rabbis? Each man for himself?

Jesus, I think you overestimate man. Man does not want to be free. He does not want to think for himself. He wants to follow...anybody. The Jews follow their Bible and their rabbis. We Romans follow Roman tradition and Roman law. You, Jesus, maybe you want to be free. But you are not like other men.

I just want everyone to have a chance to live and not be a slave.

That is a dream, Jesus. It is not real. Most men are not interested in freedom. They might say they are, but in the end they will follow somebody – anybody – like donkeys on a rope.

Perhaps you are right, Pilate. But only a free life is worth living.

What you say is dangerous, Jesus. It has the power to disturb the peace in Palestine and all over the kingdom.

All I am saying is that there must be a better world than this one. We must find it. We must create it. Is what I say wrong?

It is not wrong; it is dangerous.

Do you not agree with me, Pontius Pilate?

Pontius Pilate was not a stupid man. He did not answer Jesus's last question. He simply stared at Jesus for a few long seconds and finally told him he could go. He also told him to be careful.

TWENTY-EIGHT

When Jesus got home Mary was making bread and cooking fresh vegetables. They embraced before they spoke. Their lips were used almost as much for kissing each other as for talking to each other. When their bodies separated, Jesus poured himself a cup of wine and sat at the table. He observed the beauty and grace of Mary's body for the thousandth time. He thought she moved like a deer he had once seen in a valley near a river.

Where did you go, Jesus?

Only where I was forced to go.

What do you mean?

While you were at the market, two soldiers came and took me to see Pontius Pilate.

Being taken to Pontius Pilate is rarely a good thing.

He's not a bad man. He's just doing his job. He's

trying to keep order in Palestine.

Some men do their jobs better than others.

His job is perhaps more difficult than other jobs. He has to assuage both Rome and the Jews.

Why do you think the Romans came all the way to Palestine? Why didn't they just stay in Rome? Why would they want the problems that come with governing other lands?

Why indeed. I often think about the nature of power. Power is an odd animal. It is a bit like a vulture, except vultures prey off the dead. Power preys off the dying and the weak. The weak seek the strong. They live off each other symbiotically until the strong get weaker or the weak get stronger. Then power slips from one hand to another.

An ugly struggle.

The nature of nature! Nature can be ugly.

So what did Pilate want?

Jesus laughed.

He wanted to know if I thought I was the son of God. When I told him I had no proof of the existence of any god, he asked me if I thought I was God.

And what did you say?

I said that if there is no God, then one must decide if one should follow another man or one's own conscience.

That is why he thinks you're so dangerous, because he fears you'll follow only yourself. And he fears you'll encourage others to do the same.

That's true, Mary.

He probably fears other men will follow you whether you want it or not, and that you'll end up leading them against Rome.

I'm no leader.

You're a dreamer, Jesus. Men need a dream to follow.

Jesus laughed again.

Touché! Pilate said exactly the same thing. And I agree with both of you. Even rabbis and kings are followers. They too are slaves...slaves to their positions, slaves to their traditions, slaves to their laws.

So what is the point of trying to change anything?

That is the question I ask myself too. But deep inside me there is a burning desire to believe that some men can be free, that some men can create their own better world.

Do you know any free men?

I'm not sure.

Maybe a free man is a myth just like the gods.

You are wise and wonderful Mary. Sometimes I think that the only time I am free is when I'm loving you.

And when is that?

All the time.

Mary laughed.

Maybe love is the only real act of freedom.

Then she thought for a moment.

But maybe love is the greatest form of slavery.

Maybe it's both. Maybe freedom and slavery are the same thing. I am free to choose you, Mary Magdalene, as the one person on this earth that I love. And then, once I have chosen you, I am a slave to my love for you.

Ah, now maybe you are speaking the truth, Jesus…

I'm your slave. I need you, Mary. I need you to make the beauty of this world visible. I need you in order to feel whole. I need you to talk to. Why talk if there is no one to listen and understand? I need you to express my love. Why make love if there is no one to love? Without you, the fantastic ball of love inside me had nowhere to go. It had nothing to do. Before I met you Mary, a huge part of me was asleep. The part I now know to be the best part. Volcano-like, it had lain dormant. And then…with you…it erupted. I became whole. I was myself. The world became beautiful. Every moment there was a reason to live and move forward. The ball of my life was set in motion. Now I feel we are rolling toward infinity…Infinite love.

You know I feel the same Jesus. Love is the sun that lights the world. Love makes the world beautiful. Love lets us fly…Yes, we are slaves to our love. But without our love we are slaves to a world of darkness.

Jesus and Mary felt their loving growing stronger every day. Both sensed that only death could kill it.

TWENTY-NINE

The next morning Jesus rose with the sun and went for a walk in the square. The world was chirping and chattering; the marketplace was bustling. Jesus saw his friend John arranging the robes he was hoping to sell that day on a table.

Good morning John. Isn't it wonderful that, after sleep, the world is still here?

It's wonderful that you're still here, Jesus.

It's wonderful that the sun is still here to light up the world. Where do think it goes at night? Why does it not stay in the sky all day?

I don't know. Maybe it has other business. Maybe it has another world to light up. Maybe it sleeps like we do. And the moon…where does it go during the day?

Perhaps the sun and the moon don't like each other. When one comes, the other runs away.

Do they run or do they fly like birds?

I think they float like clouds.

And where do the clouds come from? They are as magical as the moon and sun.

It is all such an incredible mystery...Do you know, John, there is a Greek man who thinks it is the earth that is moving and that the sun is standing still? It is an amazing thought. I have heard some of the wise men in the marketplace talking.

You are the wisest man in the marketplace, Jesus. Your mind is the most open mind I know. Your thoughts begin where the thoughts of others end.

One cannot know from where one's thoughts come. The human head might be the greatest mystery of all. But then what do we know of the head of a bird or a donkey or even the head of the sun? We are so small. We are tiny specks of being in a universe that might go on forever.

But tiny doesn't mean insignificant. Countless times you've said that yourself.

That's true, John. It is a stupid mind that values things based on their size. The small can be big and the big can be small. The first can be last and the last can be first...

How big do you think the sun and moon are?

We cannot know because we don't know how far away they are.

I was talking with Paul yesterday and he thinks they can change size, like a man. They can be fat one day and small another…especially the moon. What do you think, Jesus?

I have often wondered about the size and consistency of the sun and moon. Of course, the sun is sometimes the hybrid color of fire. Other times it's pure orange or pure yellow, like certain flowers. The moon is almost always the white of one of your fine robes here. It doesn't change color as much as it changes shape. It is all such a great mystery John. Where did it all come from? What moves the moon and sun? Do they have wings? Are they the consistency of rocks? But rocks can't fly. Sometimes the sun looks to be made of fire. But fires burn out. How can the sun burn forever? Maybe they're like flowers that come and go with the seasons, except their seasons are daily.

You ask so many questions, Jesus.

Questions are far more interesting than answers. Questions stimulate the mind; answers put it to sleep.

But people want answers.

This is the problem, John. People want answers so badly that they accept any and every answer. They accept the first answer that society gives them. Even Pontius Pilate wants answers. Yesterday two soldiers took me to his palace to talk to him. He wanted to know if I thought I was the son of God.

Jesus, you're a special man. You're noticeably different from other men. Pilate knows this and so he fears you.

I am no more different than one donkey is from

another. The only difference between me and other men is that I ask more questions and am rarely satisfied with the answers I hear.

That, yes, and the fact that you love the world more than other men.

I don't know if "love" is the right word. I'm fascinated by it – fascinated by everything that exists. Existence is the greatest mystery of all. Each and every animal, plant, tree, sun, moon, person, sky, rock, and thought is a great wonder to me. I think I would use the word "love" only for the way I feel about Mary. I would use the word wonderment. Wonderment, fascination, respect for all the rest. I respect the right of everything to exist. But even the word "right" is the "wrong" word. Things don't get given "the right" to exist. Who could possibly bestow that...? Who? A god? A god that might not exist itself? Pontius Pilate? A Roman governor who happens to be in power at the moment? Things exist...that's all. Nobody gives them the right to be.

But in the world there are people who kill. Animals kill each other. What gives them the right to destroy life?

That's just it, John...nothing...nothing gives one man the right to kill another or one animal the right to kill another. It's not a matter of rights. Everything's a matter of power. Power is what runs the world. And power is a very strange thing. It comes and goes like the sun. One day it is gentle, one day it kills...just like the sun.

And who gives power to the powerful, Jesus?

Who made the sun hot, John? Probably nobody. Even if a god made the sun, it would only beg the further question, who made God? And to that question there is no answer. Finally, in the end, we can only say that existence just "is." There is no explanation for it.

But people are never satisfied with that kind of an answer.

Because, John, people are people. Be they Jews or Romans or Greeks, they want answers. Any answer is better than no answer. But not for me. And not for you.

But it's difficult to dance in the fog.

No it isn't. Not if one finds a partner to dance with. That's the meaning of love. When one loves another human being, one can live with no answers…Because love is the answer.

The two fell silent. Each was lost in his own thoughts. Finally, John spoke. *Did Pontius Pilate seem angry with you, Jesus?*

No, he seemed rather amused with me. I think he enjoyed our conversation.

You must be careful, Jesus.

That is exactly what he said as I started to leave.

Then be careful.

Be careful of whom and what?

Power…The rabbis and the Romans.

Who do you think I should fear the most, John? Our dear rabbis or our Roman conquerors?

That's a good question.

Maybe I should fear thunder and lightning and the earth when it shakes. They too have power.

But they have a different kind of power.

Are you sure, John?

With that question the two friends bade each other farewell and Jesus went walking up the hill toward the olive grove.

THIRTY

There was a rabbi on Pontius Pilate's council. He did not like Jesus of Nazareth. He kissed Pontius Pilate's ass because he wanted to save his neck in this life. He kissed Almighty Jehovah's ass because he wanted to save his neck in the next.

Rabbi, I saw the man Jesus yesterday. He came here to the palace and we talked.

And what did he say, Pontius Pilate, Honorable Ruler of Palestine?

I asked him if he thought he was the son of God. He categorically said he was not the son of God and that he wasn't sure if there was a God.

He said that...(scowls)...That is blasphemy...To deny God is the ultimate blasphemy. The next thing he will deny is your power over him.

He already has. But he did it in a rather gentle

way... (the rabbi's face has a blank look) ...He asked the question, "If there is no God, then who should a man follow?" He answered his own question by saying a man should follow his own conscience. And you know what...he's right: he should follow his own conscience. However, it's in his interest if his conscience agrees with my conscience.

Jesus has blasphemed twice, against God and the Roman Empire.

What do you think we should do with him, Rabbi? Do you think he is dangerous?

Yes.

Actually, I found him rather pleasant. I asked myself if we shouldn't use him for something to our advantage.

I can think of no way that someone who denies the existence of God can be of benefit to the earth. He's like a wild animal that cannot be trained.

But he is one of the calmest men I have ever seen.

What is calm on the outside can be fire on the inside. He's like the simmering volcano I've heard about in Pompeii. Just waiting to explode and destroy.

Destroy what?

The Kingdom of God and the Roman Empire.

But he wants no followers. How can he destroy anything if he has no followers?

The rabbi took a few seconds to think about this question. He rarely thought before he spoke. His answers were automatic. His mind was a machine.

I will talk to him, Pontius Pilate. I will find out what is in the depth of his heart. If he denies God he should have the ultimate punishment.

Death?

Of course.

Does that mean I should be put to death because I don't believe in your god Jehovah? Should all Greeks and Romans be put to death because their gods are different from yours.

The rabbi did not know what to say.

Rabbi, our Roman gods are many, some are even rather fickle and act in odd ways sometimes.

But you have your top god, Jupiter.

Why do you have only one God, one King of the universe, one Almighty Creator? Maybe many gods were needed to create the world…

The rabbi hesitated again.

Of course I have the greatest respect for you, Pontius Pilate. You are a Roman and my ruler. But this man Jesus is a Jew.

What does that matter? His birth is not his fault.

He is a traitor to the kingdom of the Jews.

But maybe he is a friend to the Romans.

The rabbi's eyes pinched almost closed.

I will talk to him, Pontius Pilate. I will see what is in his heart.

You have my leave to do so, Rabbi. Come back when you have spoken with this interesting man, this Jesus of Nazareth.

THIRTY-ONE

When Jesus was walking home from the olive grove he met Paul.

Jesus, I have just been speaking with John. I think you are going too far. With your honesty you are putting yourself in danger.

But I hurt no man nor animal. I threaten nobody.

You hurt the hearts of the rabbis and you threaten the power of Pontius Pilate.

If one little man named Jesus can hurt the hearts of the rabbis, then the rabbis' hearts are very weak.

No man likes his god attacked.

Then his god is weak and he is weaker.

Jesus, Pontius Pilate called you to his palace. That is serious. You must be concerned.

Maybe he simply wanted to talk to me, like you, John, Matthew and Mark do. Maybe he's lonely in such a large palace and in need of a friend.

This is no time to joke. He fears you are stirring up the people.

I want no followers. I want no trouble. I have done nothing wrong.

What is right for you might be wrong for Pontius Pilate…and the rabbis…

That is why men want gods…to tell them what is right and wrong. But I fear the gods are mute. It is only men speaking about what is right and wrong, men pretending they know who the gods are and what they want. But I fear the gods are all human fabrications.

But Jesus, how can you say the gods do not exist?

How can you say they do? Can you say that all gods are true? Of course not. No one thinks the Roman gods, the Greek gods, and the Jewish god are all real… Paul, all I say is that when I look at the world, I see no proof for any god or gods. I must be honest with myself. Just because the rabbis say something is true doesn't mean it is. The same goes for the Romans and the Greeks and the philosophers and the sages. Life is a great mystery. I don't know from where life came, what governs life, what moves the sun and the stars, or anything else for that matter. The only thing I know is what moves my heart.

And what is that Jesus?

Mary…Mary and the mystery of all things.

Paul froze like a statue. His eyes were blank. He shuddered himself free and spoke.

You must be careful, Jesus. You must be careful about what you say and to whom you say it.

I will say what I think. I will not hide behind a veil of lies. My only goal is to light the way to the truth.

Maybe people don't want the truth. Maybe the dark glass of this world isn't enough for them. Maybe man needs a higher world, a world behind the veil of death, suffering, and pain.

Of this, there is no doubt. But if that higher world is not real, if this world is all there is, then there is only one solution…love.

But there has to be more. There must be another world.

Why? Because the rabbis say so? Maybe the only reality is power…power and love. And love is the opposite of power. Only in love does power lose its meaning. What if, in all of our relationships, everything is just a question of power…? One man trying to get something from another…one man trying to control another…But in love this disappears…in love two people have the same goal…their desires become one…their minds and bodies fuse…there is no struggle for power because there is no separation…That is why love is so rare, Paul…because people never find another person with whom they can share the world… I have found Mary. She is my truth. She is my salvation.

Jesus looked at the blue sky and thought of Mary. His body tingled and pulsed. Paul thought of Mary, too. For Paul had no one to love.

THIRTY-TWO

When Jesus and Mary lay on their straw bed before and after making love, there were often tears of joy, and most of them fell from Jesus's eyes. This was not because Jesus was more sensitive than Mary. No, not at all. It was simply because Mary's life had been more difficult and hence, it was far easier for Jesus to feel pure happiness. Mary had been through such hell on earth that moments of pure joy were very hard to come by. Joy was always tainted by memories of suffering. Jesus had suffered little. Mary had been an orphan. She had been used and abused. She'd had to scavenge for food and drink. As a child she had not been loved. Jesus, on the other hand, had known a mother and a father who'd fed him, clothed him, and loved him. When they died, they left him with a feeling that the world could be a warm place. So when he and Mary lay together on their bed talking, tears often found their way down his face.

I cannot imagine loving anyone else like I love you, Mary.

That is how I feel about you, Jesus.

I love everything about you, everything in you, all you are and have been.

And all of me loves all of you. I never imagined such love could be possible.

Nor did I Mary. When I look at you in these moments I cannot hold back the tears that dampen my cheeks.

I love it when you cry. You are my baby.

I am your baby, your brother, your husband, and your father. I am all men to you and you are all women to me. When I suck your breast I am your child. When I hold you I am your father. When we make love I am your husband.

And you are my god.

And you, my goddess.

How can the world be so beautiful?

I don't know, but it is.

And Mary's fire was still burning. And Jesus's rod was ablaze anew. And the world was the kingdom of heaven.

THIRTY-THREE

Paul had known Mary as a harlot. Now he knew her as Jesus's lover. As he walked home, he was overcome with a jealousy that tore at every corner of his gut. He had had women, but he had never had love. His thoughts were angry and acerb:

Why does she love Jesus and not me?

How can she love a man who does not believe in God and who does not believe in another world, a world so much better than this one? This world is a hellhole, full of suffering and ugliness.

Jesus is a doubter. He is not God-fearing. What does she see in him? She must love his body. How could she love his mind?

Jesus only loves himself. He pretends that he loves other people. He pretends that he loves this world. But, no, he thinks he is God or the son of God. He thinks only of his own glory.

What is wrong with my body? Why don't women love me? Women have followed Jesus since hair started to grow on his face. He has had many women. He says he loves Mary. But that has to be a lie. I'm sure he only uses her for his pleasure. Why doesn't she love me?

What is it about Jesus that people like? His walk? His talk? His smile? Let him speak his doubts about God to the rabbis and the world. Let him tell Pontius Pilate his silly version of "truth." Let him get himself nailed to a cross...Then I'll have Mary. She is a beautiful woman. It is me she must love...No, I can't wait until Jesus is gone to have her. I will go see her tomorrow...tomorrow when she is selling her vegetables in the marketplace. I will get her to love me...She will forget about Jesus of Nazareth. She will love Paul...Paul of Palestine...One day I will establish a new religion. I will change the world...Mary and I will sit at God's side in heaven...together...forever.

Paul's plan was simple. He would first get Mary on his side. Then he would get Jesus killed. The martyr. Mankind loves martyrs. Then the most important part of his plan...he would have Mary and a few other women pretend they saw Jesus come back to life after he was dead. They would say Jesus had been resurrected. Paul would then tell the world that Jesus had died for the sins of mankind and he would promise that all weak and suffering people would get to the Kingdom of Heaven if they repented of their sins and followed him. It was a beautiful plan. The world is full of weak and suffering people. All he had to do was convince people that Jesus really was the Son of God and that His resurrection (witnessed by Mary and others) was proof. He could even say that Jesus's mother had been more than human, special, a virgin, and that God had implanted His seed in her. Then he – Paul – would marry Mary. She would love him and the world would love him because he, Paul of Palestine, had the solution for saving the world. He would, single-handedly, take the world out of its misery. He would promise a better world. And mankind would follow him because mankind was weak and paltry.

Paul's plan was lucid. He would start working on it the following morning.

THIRTY-FOUR

Mary and Jesus made love five times that night. They loved each other to life and death. Theirs was not a love of calculation. There was no "I do this for you and you do that for me." Every gesture was full of tenderness and desire. Every word they spoke to each other was truth. They were locked together like no two people had ever been locked together before. When morning came and they looked into each other's eyes, it was as if they were looking in the mirror…Mary was Jesus, Jesus was Mary, man was woman, woman was man. Man and woman had fused. And yes, one of Jesus's sperms had made its way up the river of Mary's fertile belly. A sperm and an egg had united. Creation. A baby. A child. Life…Dogs do it. Donkeys do it. Birds do it. Even trees and plants have a way of doing it. Life: it goes on and on. It is everywhere.

What is not everywhere is love. Love: Mary and Jesus. It is so rare and it can't go on and on. Why not? Death. It too is everywhere.

THIRTY-FIVE

Paul let the sun rise above the treetops before going to find Mary in the marketplace. He had hardly slept that night, with his plan firing through his head. Never before had he felt such excitement.

Good morning, my dear Mary.

Morning Paul.

How's business? Your vegetables always look the finest in the market.

I'm not sure about that.

You're also the most beautiful of the vegetable sellers.

There is only one man who truly appreciates my beauty.

No Mary, you are mistaken on two accounts…I too appreciate your beauty and Jesus is only using you for his own satisfaction.

How can you say such a thing, Paul? You know nothing about the love Jesus and I have for each other.

But I do know what kind of a man Jesus is. He doubts the existence of God. He does not believe in truth. He fears no other man, not even Pontius Pilate or the rabbis.

That is partly why I love him. He's a man, not a mouse.

But Mary, such a man is only trouble. He will soon be put to death. Your love will be in vain. Don't you see? You should love me, not Jesus. A man who does not love God, cannot truly love a woman.

How can you say such things about your friend? You, Paul, are not a friend, you're a traitor. You don't know Jesus like I know him.

When he's dead, we'll talk again.

Stop suggesting he'll die.

He must stop suggesting there's no God.

He doesn't say there's no God. He says he has seen no proof of a god. He says the Romans have their gods, the Greeks have their gods, and the Jews have their One Almighty God. He says some of these gods must be false. It is possible they all are.

But Mary, a man like Jesus goes against the grain. He walks alone. He will die alone.

No. When he dies, my heart will die with him. We are one. We are a single body of love.

Paul could see that he was getting nowhere with Mary. She would have to wait. He would go find the rabbi who sat on Pontius Pilate's council.

Well Mary, I must be going. The days are getting shorter. Winter is coming.

Goodbye Paul.

Goodbye Mary and think on my words.

I already have.

The man who would found the Christian Church walked off moving left and right as he made his way through the crowds.

THIRTY-SIX

The rabbi didn't need to be convinced that Jesus was a dangerous man; he had thought it for years.

Paul, my friend, any man who doubts the existence of God is a threat not only to Palestine, but to the world.

Yes.

And what I fear the most is that Jesus is sure that he himself is God.

It's not clear, Rabbi. Sometimes he says he is God and sometimes he says he is the Messiah that the Jews have been waiting for. I think he has hallucinations. In any case I heard him in the marketplace yesterday saying that if there was no life after death – if there was no God – then we must worship this life…He started stirring the people with his charisma. He told them that they should be slaves to nobody – neither rabbi nor

Roman!

His charisma makes him all the more dangerous. I'll tell Pilate immediately. We, as Jews, must protect our kingdom, and Pontius Pilate, as the ruler of Palestine, must protect the safety of our land.

At least Paul's day had not been wasted. The rabbi would inform Pilate that things were getting worse, that Jesus was trying to incite the masses. This, of course, was a total lie. Jesus never preached his ideas; he revealed them only to a few close friends. The one thing that was partially true was that Jesus believed that if there was no life after death, then this world took on ultimate value…to waste this life would become the greatest sin of all. But Jesus also knew that men were perhaps no freer than animals or the moon and sun. They were what they were and they could not be otherwise. The world could not be saved. It would always be what it was: a great machine that man was simply a part of that turned and turned and could never be stopped. Man would always have false gods and false prophets and strange values. That was man and he would never crawl out of his hole and into the light of a so-called "truth." Man was like a blind bat flying frantically in the night trying to find a home that didn't exist. Mankind was as innocent as any infant ever born.

Paul would never have Mary. He would find other women to help him carry out his plan, weak women to whom love was as foreign as it was to him.

THIRTY-SEVEN

Darling Jesus, I have been looking everywhere for you.

I was walking in the olive grove and thinking about our love. The world has taken on a different glow since I met you. I used to see much more ugliness; now I see much more beauty.

What one sees is always a function of what is inside the body that has the gazing eyes. Our love has changed the colors and texture of the world. I love you. I love the world.

I love us. I love our world.

But there is a part of our world that I do not love today, Jesus. Your friend Paul came to me in the marketplace this morning. He tried to tell me that I was wasting my love on you. He wanted to pull me from you. He said you were a dangerous man and that you would surely die soon.

Such behavior doesn't surprise me at all. Paul is a sad man, a weak man. He does not have the strength to understand or appreciate our love. I don't think he knows what it is to love another person. I find that sad.

He is a dangerous man. He wants to destroy the most beautiful thing on earth... Our love.

I don't know if he ever will feel real love. It's not something one can teach to another. It must grow and blossom within one's own heart.

I told Paul that he knew nothing about the feelings we have for each other.

And you're right. A love like ours is one of the rarest things on this earth. There is only one sun; perhaps there is only one Mary-and-Jesus.

And it's sad because love is what can make the world a better place.

Yes. People who love respect the rest of the world. Look at us. We wake up every morning so grateful to be alive. We can't wait to see the sun and have another day together on earth. We love life. People like Paul don't love this world at all. They dream of another world. That is why they create all their gods: to save them from "this life." This is my only real message to the world: the kingdom of God is not in the next life, it is here...now. This life is the only life we can be sure of. All the gods and afterlives might be pure chimera, creations of sick minds and sick people.

Yes, Jesus. God must be inside each man, each

creature, each existing thing.

You are wise, wonderful, and beautiful, Mary. I love you to death. And where there is love, there is life. God is love. God is life.

Mary and Jesus fell into each other's arms and onto the straw bed. They could do nothing else. When they finished making love, it was usually Jesus who spoke first. This time it was Mary.

Jesus, darling, your friend Paul is convinced that you are in danger because of your ideas.

Paul's my friend because I am friends with all men. He is the reason I am in danger. He spreads falsehoods about my ideas. He neither understands me nor my vision of the world.

Neither do most men.

The longer I live, the more I think that's true. Most people's eyes cannot see very far. It's not their fault. They are weak and so are their eyes. Lately I have been thinking about how people always want to see a cause and a creator behind everything. They want a reason for everything. The world must have a reason! Life must have a reason! Everything that happens must have a reason. When lightning strikes the earth, people want to say, "Ah, it is an act of God…God is angry with man because of something he has done." But it is very possible that God has absolutely nothing to do with the lightning. The lightning might simply be caused by an infinity of things in nature. When there is a flood, the rabbis say that God is punishing man for his sins. But maybe the flood has nothing to do with God and sin. People want simple answers for everything. That is the way the human mind works. It wants simple causes, simple connections, simple dichotomies like good and evil. And Mary, it is very possible that man sees the world in a way that is completely false.

I have thought the same...

Perhaps God is not the cause of anything. Perhaps there was no creation like the Bible says. Perhaps there is no good and evil like the Bible says. Perhaps the whole universe is a big machine that has been turning forever and will continue to turn forever. Perhaps man is just a tiny cog in the great wheel of existence. Perhaps thunder just happens like everything else just happens. Of course, one can find reasons, but what are the reasons behind those reasons? And the reasons behind those reasons? Perhaps everything is infinitely and eternally linked together. Perhaps all causes are built into the nature of the world.

But Jesus, men can't think this way. They must have their gods. When things go wrong, they must have their evil and their guilty.

And because they don't love this life, they must have their world-after-this-world. Yes. Men can't imagine that this world might simply exist without a cause or a reason. They cannot imagine that the earth, moon and stars have no beginning and no end and no higher reason for existing. But it is very possible that there is no ultimate cause for anything. Everything might just be. Man, monkey, moon, water, wheat, wine, weather, grass, stars, kings, slaves, fish and insects all linked together…all nature…all together… alone…because there is nothing else that can be…

Most people cannot fathom such thoughts.

So I ask myself if I am dangerous…and if I am in danger…

You are not dangerous, Jesus. You love life. Life is a miracle for you. You respect the biggest and the smallest creatures. But you must be careful about Paul. He is trying to create trouble for you. Of that I'm sure.

Paul is like thunder and lightning or a coiled and poisonous snake. His actions could be nefarious, but… so are many other things in the world.

You must be vigilant, my love.

I will. But if the authorities come back and ask questions, I will tell them the truth.

But the truth is dangerous.

That is why I keep it to myself most of the time. But Mary, the real the truth is that I don't even pretend to know the truth. What I think I do know is that the way most men see the world is probably very un-true. It's the lies of the world that are dangerous. The lies of the world that act like fences for sheep. To keep the sheep inside. The lies keep the masses under control…But then again, maybe the fences are necessary? Maybe truth really is the most dangerous thing for mankind. Maybe Paul and the rabbis are right…maybe I am dangerous…,

I'm worried Jesus. I'm worried they'll take you from me.

To separate us would be the greatest tragedy I can imagine.

Yes.

The only thing that can break our love is death.

And that's why we treasure our lives.

I love you Mary Magdalene.

I love you Jesus of Nazareth.

THIRTY-EIGHT

The next morning Jesus decided to go to the marketplace to find Paul. As he was walking through the crowd, an old woman fell to the ground in front of him, dropping her basket. She lay motionless.

She's dead! someone shouted.

She has been stricken by the devil! another called.

A crowd gathered around the old woman and stared. Jesus knelt down beside her and took her right hand. He gently rubbed the palm and the fingers. Then he bent forward and ran his fingers through her grizzled, matted grey hair.

Bless you, he said softly. *May life continue to breathe inside you.*

A few seconds later the woman opened her eyes. She saw Jesus and said, *Where am I?*

You are in Nazareth. You are still on this beautiful

earth, Jesus answered.

The woman's lips slowly separated and a delicate smile appeared.

He has saved her, a man shouted. *Jesus has performed another miracle! He has saved this old woman from the arms of death!* It was the voice of Paul who had pushed his way through the crowd.

Jesus said nothing. He and another man helped the woman to her feet. A young girl gathered the things that had fallen from her basket.

Are you okay? Jesus asked.

I think so. I don't know what happened. I suddenly felt like I had no blood in my head.

Hopefully you'll be fine. Can you walk alone?

I will walk with her, the little girl said.

And what's your name? Jesus asked.

Romée.

What a lovely name. Are you from Rome?

Where is that? the girl asked. She was half Jesus's size, probably six or seven years old.

Rome is where the emperor lives. It is far away in the direction of where the sun comes every morning. Many soldiers come from there. Is your father a soldier?

I am a child of the world. My mother says the world is my father.

Your mother is wise. We are all children of this world. We are all children of God. It is good of you to walk with this woman to be sure she is all right.

The old woman looked at Jesus, then took the little

girl's hand.

Jesus of Nazareth, you truly are a man of God, she said.

Many in the crowd had listened to this conversation. Now everyone began to disperse. People chattered about the miracle they had witnessed. Paul came and stood close to Jesus.

Why call it a miracle, Paul? You know it wasn't. I didn't bring her back to life. She never died.

People need miracles, Paul said.

I came to the market looking for you. We must talk.

And they talked. But talking did nothing to change Paul's vision of the world or how he saw himself and Jesus therein.

THIRTY-NINE

The smell. The mind. The past. The touch. The skin. The blemishes. The feet. The way he or she makes love. The nose, eyes, fingers, arms, legs, hair, belly, mouth, shape, nape, when asleep and awake. The sound of the voice. What the voice utters. The walk, talk, and smile. Have you ever known another person about whom you loved everything? Absolutely everything.

This was the case with Jesus and Mary. The world was about to destroy this love. The world did not know that such a love was possible. Not Pontius Pilate. Not the rabbis. Certainly not Paul, John, Luke, or Matthew or any other of Jesus's friends. No one understood how Mary and Jesus felt about each other. There might be other such couples later on as the world spun its lonely path through space. Romeo and Juliet. Tristan and

Isolde. Elizabeth Taylor and Richard Burton. John and Yoko…Who knows? But up until 0 AD there had never been a love like the love Jesus and Mary had for each other.

When Jesus was sentenced to die on the cross with a few other local petty thieves, the absurdity and stupidity of the world was at what one might call "an ordinary zenith." Paul continued to spread rumors that Jesus was the Messiah and a performer of miracles. The rabbi who advised Pontius Pilate thought Jesus was a threat to the stability of Palestine and was loosening the rabbinical hold on the hearts and minds of the people. Pontius Pilate, though even a bit fond of Jesus, didn't really care much either way and, for him, sending a man to his death was not much different than taking a pee. Life was not worth much. And it still isn't. Today some people give value to certain aspects of life: community, large mammals, money, cars, gods, sports teams, large houses, jewelry…But few people, if any, give value to all that exists. The whole universe never gets the same status as the local shit. Small animals never get the status of large ones. Animals are never up with people. Trees, flowers, and all that grows from the ground never get the status of creatures with blood. Rocks and dirt always lag behind so-called "living" things. This has always made people like Jesus chuckle because rocks and moons and planets have been around for millions and billions of years, but they're not considered alive.

Sure, there have been pockets of people who respected more than the average Joe...some tribes of American Indians, Buddhists, and maybe a few others. But all in all the people of the world have never been very nice to the whole of existence. And their glorious gods have always tended to exacerbate the problem.

So, to put it simply, there was only one Christian and he died on the cross. What came after him had little or nothing to do with his vision of the world. What came to be called Christianity was not about Jesus Christ. It was the work of a weak sad man named Paul. It should have been called Paulianity. Paul did not love life or the world. And the world did not love him. He used Jesus to create a world wherein he had a place, wherein he became important. But this was not Jesus's world. In Jesus's world there was no concept of sin or the devil. Nobody was sacrificed for the sins of the world. There was no heaven or hell or judgment day. There was no virgin mother. There was no resurrection of the dead, no hate of the body, no belief in an eternal soul. All these things came from the unhappy mind of a man who did not love this world.

When Pontius Pilate called Jesus back to his palace a second time, the eggs were already fried. The rabbi had convinced the governor of Palestine that Jesus was a nuisance. He was getting people to think for themselves. This has always been a danger for those in power.

Jesus did not believe in things unseen. But neither

did he believe that the human mind was, necessarily, capable of grasping the truth. And maybe the truth was like a serpent that could bite itself in the butt.

Jesus simply respected life. All life. Being. The whole bag of marbles. He didn't pick and choose what was of value. Everything was of value. He didn't claim to know where the world came from. He didn't claim to know what was behind the world. He didn't claim to know what caused what. He had no idea if the mind was free or if the whole idea of *free will* was a human invention that had absolutely nothing to do with reality. It was all a great mystery to him.

In the end, Jesus knew two things:

Life is rampant and death is rampant. Both beauty and tragedy are everywhere. In such a world it is hard for a thinking man not to go crazy.

If there's a god, its name should be Love. His love for Mary was his salvation.

Jesus carried the cross to the top of the hill. As soon as he set it down, the Roman soldiers told him lie on his back on top of it. He stared at the empty blue sky as the soldiers tied his body to the wood. Then they drove spikes through his wrists and ankles. It took four soldiers to lift the cross and plant it in a hole in the ground. The petty thieves got the same treatment.

This barbarism is the image that Paul used to define his religion. He could have used the image of Jesus and Mary in each other's arms the night before in the throes of ecstasy as they made love for the last time. Had Jesus made a religion, this is probably what he would have done.

Jesus said a few things on the cross…*Forgive them for they know not what they do…The kingdom of God is here and now within you…*that kind of thing. But, of course, all that got lost in the shuffle of history as Christianity expanded with Islam, Buddhism, and Hinduism and locked its arms around a good part of the world.

Night was coming. The moment Jesus expired, Mary was the only person at the foot of the cross. Paul and the others had left hours before when their friend had stopped talking. Mary lay on her back and stared at the same sky Jesus had looked at that morning as he was being attached to the two wooden planks. As the heavens darkened a few scattered stars were beginning to twinkle. Mary had brought the tattered blanket under which she and Jesus had slept during the last three years of his life on the earth. She curled her body inside it placing both hands on her slightly inflated belly. Before she was asleep, one hand crawled out to wipe away the few final drops of blood that fell on the face that the dead man had so adored.

ABOUT THE AUTHOR

Jon Ferguson was born in October 1949 in Oakland, California, into a devout Christian family, much like his favorite philosopher, Friedrich Nietzsche. In fact, as a child, church services were held in the family living room. At age 17, his enthusiasm for sport was almost usurped by a keenness to save the world when he enrolled at the Mormon-owned Brigham Young University. Little by little, though, he realized that if Jesus couldn't do it, neither could he. His faith in God began to crumble.
With an adieu to the US academic world where he'd been immersed in anthropology and philosophy – and with a desire to engage with the world at large – Ferguson hopped on a plane in 1973 and by chance ended up in Nyon, Switzerland where he was soon playing basketball in the top Swiss league, becoming a key player in what fans consider to have been the golden age.
Half a century later, still in Switzerland, he is now just as well known for his writing (eighteen books published in French) as for his coaching (thirty years' worth). He won more games than any coach in Swiss basketball history, but he likes to remind people that he lost more than everyone else as well... He has written over twenty novels and a book on Nietzsche, Nietzsche au Petit Déjeuner ("Nietzsche for Breakfast") and a book on the history of Swiss basketball, Of Hoops and Men. For twenty-five years he also wrote a bi-weekly column in the Lausanne newspaper called "Ainsi Parla Schmaltz". His novel Farley's Jewel (Cinco Puntos Press, 1998) won a Barnes & Noble "Discover Great New Writers of America" prize.
Find out more:
www.jonferguson.com

BOOKS BY JON FERGUSON

(Published by Huge Jam, 2022)

Adam's Cane
Foster's Depression
The Last Day Forever
Jesus & Mary
Mary & God
God & Naomi

Download 'The Last Day Forever' for free from the author's website
www.jonfergusonbooks.com

Out soon by the same author:

The Old Man and the Stone
Farmer's Daughter
Don't Bullshit Me Daddy
The Anthropologist

www.hugejam.com
www.jonfergusonbooks.com